DIRTY DEALS A DARK MAFIA ROMANCE SERIES

(MICHELI MAFIA) BOOK 5

ZOE BETH GELLER

KINKY INK PUBLISHING

Dirty Deals
Dirty: A Dark Mafia Romance
(Micheli Mafia) Book 5

By Zoe Beth Geller
Kinky Inc Publishing

Cover design by Shepard Originals

Edited by: Shelley's Editing Services

❀ Created with Vellum

FREE SAMPLE OF ITALIAN KING

Free Chapters Italian King
https://geni.us/ItalianKingSample

GLOSSARY

GLOSSARY

Basta - that's enough

Buon Compleanno - Happy Birthday

Buongiorno – good morning

Capisci - you understand

Capisco - I understand

Ciao - hello, bye-bye

Ciao, come sta? - Hello, how are you?

Chiuso - closed

Cretino - idiot, stupid

D'enotti - of unknown origin (parentage)

Due espresso, per favore - two espresso, please

Familigia - family

Gelato - ice cream with higher fat content

Mangia - eat

Nessun problema - no problems

Niente - nothing

Normalmente - normally

Perfetto - perfect

Piazza - square, place
Polizia - police
Pronto - ready (used to answer the telephone)
Salute - health
Sì – yes
Va bene - all right, okay

PLAYLIST

Play list for Dirty Deals
https://open.spotify.com/playlist/4swp9yeiqY934jcfKpTFcp
My Universe by Coldplay, BTS
Butter by BTS
My girl by Jackson Penn
Don't Mess with my Mind by EMO
Secrets by One Republic
Complicated by Avril Lavigne

1

___

RICCARDO

I lost my wingman, Dante, to his lovely wife, but he's still my boss and someone I count on. I'm amused sitting in his den smoking cigars, he's changed so much. The playboy is gone while I'm still sleeping alone and living a life free of attachments.

"Dante, what are we gonna do about Ignazio?" I ask from the comfort of a well-worn leather chair. Over his shoulder, I notice something new. A heart-shaped silver frame holding a picture of his recent wedding sitting on a shelf and an antique bookcase. It concerns me because a man in love creates new liabilities. It's not enough to keep himself safe, he needs to keep her safe, too.

It's not easy to do when Dante owns and operates legitimate and illegitimate businesses. Last year, someone tried to make it look like he killed two rivals. We managed to clear his name, but it's not over.

"We'll never be safe until we track her down," he answers, clearly resolved to find a fitting end to the bitch as his eyes narrow with the thought of her.

I've finally weaned myself off the cigs. It wasn't easy. I

puff out circles of smoke and watch them float on a slight breeze. Now it's an occasional cigar with the guys. Juliet would have our hides for smoking in the house, so the shutters are open. The sun set hours ago; the night air is chilly, but I find it refreshing.

"Oh, by the way, Juliet is expecting. It's early, so we're not making an announcement until later." Dante grins.

I'm not surprised. When he met Juliet, it was pretty much curtains for his bachelor lifestyle. I'm happy for him, but a baby is one more person to keep safe, and that's more work for me.

"Congratulations." After doing the math, "Hmmm, practically a honeymoon baby," I point out.

"Close, you know, it's been a long time for you. You might want to consider getting a woman to settle down with; you're still young." Dante lets his back arch in a second of relaxation. His father's large, overstuffed office chair has a squeaky spring, and it protests under his shifting weight.

"Hmm, never thought much about it; I'm set in my ways. Besides, we have this nasty Ignazio business to deal with," I puff on my cigar deep in thought. I lean forward, my legs anchoring my sturdy frame. "What is she doing in Moscow? There has to be a mafia connection. Who else would house a psychopath?"

"Actually, the latest intel from Giovi in Sicily is that she's moved to St. Petersburg."

Giovi's father was one of two men killed in an attempt to set Dante up for murder. Like Dante, Giovi is seeking revenge. Both men need to protect their families and fortunes. It's the mafia way.

"St. Petersburg?" I all but swallow my cigar.

Fuck! I have someone close to me living there. This can't be good.

Ignazio has a laundry list of aliases. There's no telling what name she's using in Russia. She missed her calling in life. She would have made an excellent operative. Being independent doesn't mean she gets to keep and use all her ill-gotten gains at her discretion. Clearly, she has no problem killing for profit; the bodies are piling up. She was lying low. Now she's surfaced, is it an indication she's focusing on her next target? Or baiting us?

The blood must've drained from my face because Dante asks, "Are you okay?" His question brings me back to the present, and I remember we all need to stay on our toes and rid the planet of this woman.

"My ward, Liat, is with a dance troupe in St. Petersburg. I didn't want her to go there, but she's convinced the Russians can teach her things, making her a prima ballerina." I shake my head.

She needs to return to Italy.

Liat became my responsibility after her parents and my wife were killed in Tel Aviv. A lifetime ago, I rescued her and kept her hidden from any enemies, and I hope— the Phantom. I no longer work for the elite Israeli intelligence agency, so I assumed the danger was over.

Now, our number one enemy is in Russia. Is it fate or coincidence my last deal was rumored to have involved a Russian group?

Fuck me.

What if Ignazio goes after Liat to get to me? Why? What have I done other than working for Dante to draw her wrath? I'm getting ahead of myself. There is no evidence Ignazio knows anything about me or my past.

And the pope isn't Catholic.

"I hope it's a coincidence she's in the same city as Liat. This can't be happening again," I groan, leaning forward to stab my smoldering stogie into the ashtray, pretending it's Ignazio's face.

"What do you remember from Tel Aviv? Is it possible she was there?" Dante stands and proceeds to pace back and forth across the expensive Persian rug.

"I have no clue. I mean, there was someone named Phantom who facilitated the gun deal between the Russians and the insurgents. As you know, I could never identify who it was."

"Ignazio would have been. . ."

"Early twenties. That was twenty years ago. Liat was five at the time; now she's twenty-five."

"No trace?" Dante stops briefly before he returns to his chair.

"None. And you know how well I do my homework."

"I do. She's a formidable opponent with many escape routes. The weather in Russia is nasty right now. The land-scape is covered in dirty snow and will be melting."

"We have to go to her turf. This sucks balls," I groan.

"Yes, it does."

Dante leans forward, snuffing his cigar out in the marble ashtray sitting on his oversized desk. "Are you up for this?" We lock eyes, both determined to get this done.

I stand. "Of course. First, we need to make sure your family is safe. Then, we need to get prepared for battle. It won't be easy. We'll use our connections to smuggle in weapons and drugs to pave the way. Probably some cognac, the more expensive, the better, according to Giovi. We need lots of money, Cryptocurrency, fake IDs. . ."

"Francesca is handling the IDs."

I nod. The woman is a worthy adversary. I'm happy she's on our team.

"Great, I'll formulate a plan and call a family meeting," Dante's casual tone fills the room.

"Giovi wants to go," I promised the man I'd float it out for Dante to decide.

"Hmm, let me think on it," we shake hands before I swipe my DB sunglasses off his desk, "I'm heading home."

"Sure," he walks with me to the front door.

"As always, tell your mother thanks for the lovely Sunday dinner."

"For sure." Dante nods, closing the door behind me.

I OPEN my bedroom shutters to let in the night air. It's March, spring is around the corner. Plants begin to emerge, and the bare trees sprout fresh leaves, symbolizing new life. When the trees fill in, the tourist and the brick sidewalks welcome the shade. The summer heat is brutal, and Florence sidewalks are hotter than a pizza oven.

I'm not one to care much about the weather. I've traveled so much that it doesn't matter to me. However, St. Petersburg will be cold. In case I die in the frozen tundra, I need to call Liat and convince her to live with my sister here in Italy until this business is over.

I crawl into bed naked, the soft sheets caressing my body for lack of a woman's touch.

I hate nighttime and wrestle with sleep as if it's a demon. I glance at the prescription bottle filled with pills on my nightstand. As much as I hate them, they provide relief when I wake up drenched in sweat in the middle of the night. I sit, take a deep breath, and hope it calms the panic squeezing my lungs.

They say time heals all wounds. I say, for some, there is

not enough time. Time to live, rejoice, to have a second chance with the woman I love is gone forever.

I'm a cynical man haunted by memories of the fateful evening in Tel Aviv. I can't forget the sound of the explosion or the scene of the aftermath. I failed my wife. I failed them all.

My job is to keep Dante and his family safe. I keep everyone else at a distance. It's easier to be alone than to risk losing someone again. I worry the past will repeat itself. My diligence and lack of dependents afford me the time to be vigilant.

I was a broken man when Dante discovered me at his favorite café while getting his morning coffee. A few words, numerous cups of coffee, and his intuitive instincts made us peers.

He didn't ask many questions, only if I would work for him and his father. I didn't need the money. It didn't take long for me to decide working would be a healthy alternative to drinking and smoking myself to death.

Now he's married, it increases the risk of a potential strike. We hired more guards because women, and children are no longer off-limits to our enemies. With this in mind, Dante prefers to resolve matters amicably whenever possible.

I never see myself getting married. I intend to remain free of entanglements. To keep my sister and my ward safe, I limit physical contact with them.

I'm not one to use unnecessary words or show a lot of emotion to communicate, and it's been easy to keep to myself. It's what I know.

For years I was depressed and wanted to kill myself to escape the guilt. At times, my isolation from the world makes me a miserable son of a bitch.

Not only did I lose my beloved Alana, but also my best friends, Levi and Rebekah Tal. I was supposed to meet them at the theater to see Liat dance her first solo.

Traffic never moves fast in Tel Aviv. I left work late, sending them off without me. My partner tried calling Levi to warn him he may have been compromised. Levi uncovered information about a new gun trafficking ring in Russia run by someone named Phantom.

I have no idea who was behind the heinous car bomb. By the time we reached the explosion scene, their car was unrecognizable, and I immediately knew everyone was dead.

Was I the intended target? It's my fault. Everyone I cared about, died. I wasn't a stranger to crime rings, being an intelligence officer. Maybe I will get some closure in St. Petersburg.

2

———

LIAT

"Riccardo, I don't understand. Why are you flipping out? Everything is fine here," I protest on our video call as I snap a pencil in my hand. Doesn't he know how hard it is to get into this dance troupe?

"It's not safe. You need to come home," he commands. He's stubborn even if he has my best interest at heart.

However, I have dreams of Broadway, and this is my ticket to New York. "You're being overprotective. The only person I need to watch out for is Chloe."

"Chloe from Paris?" His eyebrows pull together as he mulls this information over for a minute.

"The very same," I mumble. It's old news and it won't die a normal death. Since high school in France, she's been riding my ass when we both competed for the lead part in productions. It's ironic she's here in St. Petersburg with me. If I could sleep with one eye open, I would.

It's a big world, but the ballet world is small, and I continually run into the same faces. Aleksandr is an incredible dancer, and he's a great partner. We spent hours practicing for the spring performance of *Sleeping Beauty*.

"I'm coming to visit you soon, and you'll be leaving with me."

I let out a heavy sigh. Then I unleash on him in Italian, telling him I've worked too hard not to dance in the performance. I need to have this experience on my resume.

"Liat." His voice all but rattles the long narrow windows of my flat. "I'll talk to you when I see you. When is your performance opening?"

"Next week."

"Fine. Text me the dates. I'll be there on opening night. Don't make any new friends, and be careful."

"Careful of what?" My heart skips a beat. He's a security expert, and he's never been so pushy with me. "What's going on, Riccardo?"

"I'll fill you in soon."

"Okay." There's my cue to shut up because others might hear our conversation. "Love you, Riccardo." I play off the spat for whoever is eavesdropping on our call. Two can play this game.

"Okay. Talk later. And don't break a leg," he warns.

"Very funny," I reply, knowing he's mocking me. Anyone who watched the movie *Red Sparrow* knows it's bad luck. As long as Chloe waits in the wings, I don't want to jinx anything. God forbid. I have enough to worry about in the vicious world of dance moms and the children they had so that they could relive their life vicariously through them. Most of the girls are now grown, like me, and I've noticed not all of them turned out to be fully functioning adults.

Fear, colder than a Siberian winter, comes over me. I worry something might befall me. Even though Riccardo was my guardian, I grew up with his sister, Vivian. He has been elusive most of my life. Joy doesn't come close to describing how I felt when he showed up on Christmas or

Easter. Birthdays were met with lavish gifts, but he never stayed long. His job, his life... a mystery.

I've had a crush on him my entire life. It's silly to idolize him the way I do. To impress him, I'd wear my best dress when he would visit, but I don't think he ever noticed. He'll always see me as a skinny little girl who needs someone to watch over her.

Maybe my desire stems from the loneliness and desolation I felt as a child when we left the Middle East. Instinctively, I knew he'd be lost to the world and consumed by his grief if he lost me. We flew to Rome and didn't stop until we made it to the Italian countryside. There, I met his sister and her family, who raised me.

Riccardo didn't talk much when I was a child, nor does he speak much now; he prefers to listen. He became my immediate family overnight. Is it so wrong for me to still want him? Or, is he a substitute for my father?

His salt-and-pepper hair and beard are the most apparent indication he's older than me. According to his posture, he is a man bad guys don't mess with. He stands tall, and his commanding presence is similar to a soldier or a Carabiniere. He's not insecure, that's for damn sure.

On occasion, I've seen his eyes light up, like when he bought me a set of designer luggage for boarding school. I almost cried. Aunt Vivian wanted me to stay home and be a normal child. It's the only time I heard them argue. He said it wasn't up to them to mold me into what they wanted. I had to find myself and pursue my dream.

God knows we all deserve some respite from the horrors of life. I was shocked he stuck up for me. I was twelve at the time. Riccardo knew how important ballet was to me. Knowing my famous mother, how could he be the one to stand in my way when he knew her best? I don't remember much of my life in Israel. What five-year-old would?

My mother was a dancer. It was only a matter of time before I naturally fell into the footsteps of one parent or the other. It's possible Riccardo was grateful I wasn't planning on joining the military.

True to form, Riccardo drilled the Paris Ballet Academy on their security protocols and made a few improvements before he left me to settle into my dorm. He rarely smiles. As a child, the only time he held me was when he picked me up from the recital that fateful day. He wanted me to be independent and didn't coddle me. In retrospect, it might be why I'm not as fearful as others who didn't have such a traumatic beginning.

I hid my disappointment when he left. He's always leaving. I thought we were a pair of misfits, and together, we made a whole person. We were both broken and in need of love. We still are to this day.

I can't wait to see him. It's been months. I wonder if he'll always be the same, a man whose eyes are untrusting and his heart—closed.

"Liat." Aleksandr knocks. He hollers at my door, "Let's go for pizza," when I don't answer immediately.

I live in an apartment complex with walls thinner than tissue paper if that's possible. The entire troupe is housed together, and most share their living quarters. I get to have my own small flat. This is the first time I've truly lived in my own place.

"I'm coming," I unlock the door. Aleksandr huffs as he's out of breath when he barges in.

"What's up?" He's only twenty and the best there is in the Russian ballet. He's tall with dark brown hair and bright eyes the color of sapphires.

"We're going out to eat, come, come," his voice rushes as much as his words.

"Why haven't I heard about it?"

"Because we're going to bust Chloe eating pizza," he snickers.

"What? The ice queen herself? I have to see this."

"Right?"

I grab my coat from the hook. There is no closet in this tiny studio and no walls to separate the kitchen from the dining room. To feel better about my small flat, I tell myself it's how people live in New York.

"Ready." I smile impishly as he opens the door, and we walk to the closest pizzeria, where we join our interpreter, George. He was born in Moscow and is a linguist. He's quite handsome.

"George," I call out when we arrive.

"Hi, Liat. She's here," he says giving me a quick glance. After that, he never takes his eyes off the large storefront window.

Oh, boys and their pranks.

"Who's going to snap the picture?"

"You can," Aleksandr suggests too quickly.

"I'm not crazy; she'll piss on my ballet shoes."

"Right, then, George, it's you."

"Me? Why me?" George protests, but his smile gives it away. He's such a prankster. It comes naturally to him.

"Because you can get away with these things, and no one blames you. Besides, we need you. Just remember to delete it from your phone and post it under your anonymous account from the dark web."

"How do you know about computer stuff?" Aleksandr sends me a quizzical look.

"I live here; I hear things," I reply smugly and shrug it off.

I sneak a peek inside the restaurant as I stand behind George. "She's almost finished an entire medium pizza!"

George checks his phone to make sure the flash isn't on, and after we hear the shutter click, we dash to the burger joint around the corner. My heart is racing. It's a childish prank, but Chloe deserves it. She has a way of irritating everyone. When she's not getting enough attention, she sucks the joy out of every occasion.

Complain, complain, complain. It should be her middle name.

"I got it," George's energetic voice is infectious, and we giggle. He passes his phone to Aleksandr, and then to me.

"She's going to be so pissed," I murmur.

"She's a bitch, and you know it," Aleksandr adds emphatically.

"Yeah, but she's not going to be happy when she hears about this. I don't want her coming after me. However, a picture of her in the bathroom puking it up would be priceless," I snicker.

The guys chuckle. I've always been more comfortable around men than girls. Maybe it's because I got my fill of drama at dance classes. I've had years of mothers and daughters thinking they were princesses.

"Relax, it will be fun," George says. "I gotta go; you two eat. I'll see you tomorrow."

"Bye," I reply, but it's pointless. He's gone before the words leave my mouth.

Is this an excuse for Aleksandr to get me alone? He's flirtatious. I've kept it a secret somehow, but I've never been with a man. I don't know how the guys know; I heard years ago it's the way I walk; I don't believe it.

Aleksandr is my best friend, and George is the jester of the bunch. He's brilliant, though, being a linguist. Nowadays, no matter where you are in the world, someone in the bus line or grocery store knows some English.

Aleksandr and I wait in line to place our food order at the register, grab a drink from a machine, and sit at a table for two. It's not uncommon to share tables here, but it would be in Italy.

I sip my soft drink through a paper straw, and our eyes meet.

"So, what's up? You were out of breath earlier. You, okay?"

"Oh, yeah. Just happy to see you outside of work. Nothing new," he replies.

"You're sweet," I murmur and avoid eye contact.

"Just what every guy wants to hear," he teases, but behind his words is a vibe that warns me—he wants more.

Our food is up, and I'm saved from getting cornered as I tell him my guardian is coming to see our performance.

"That's great. Are you nervous?"

"I don't think so. I'm in a different place when I dance."

"I know what you mean. It's a great escape for me."

"How so?"

He appears nervous and fidgets with his fries. He avoids eye contact and glances around the room. He shrugs his shoulders as if he's indifferent. "It's nothing. I've applied to go to the States, but I don't know if I'll get a visa."

"Why not?" I take a bite out of my burger. I'll burn this off tomorrow at practice.

"It's very political here," his voice is low, and he clams up. A chill runs up my spine. I'm afraid to ask questions. I know I can't speak of certain things in public. Men are patrolling the streets who belong to the Russian equivalent of America's CIA. The people here can't trust anyone, especially in public.

I change the topic. "This burger is fantastic." I take another bite.

"It is," he agrees and seems to relax, leaving me to wonder what is going on.

This odd incident makes me happy Riccardo is coming soon. Maybe I bit off more than I could chew by coming here.

3

———

RICCARDO

Liat is overconfident. She's stubborn and willful. Maybe I should have been in her life more as a child. I left her thinking I probably gave her the best gift of her life. I'm not suitable for relationships. I'm shrouded in a cloud of death where women are concerned.

I drive my BMW to Dante's as it begins to rain. I pray it's not an omen for our next task at hand. I'm not a religious man, so praying is out.

I wonder if Hercules ever got tired of wandering for ten years. It's been a long fifteen for me. Granted, I'm in one place, but what do I have to go home to? I'm getting older. Time catches up to us all. Do all men in their forties think about their future?

No. But most men aren't in organized crime either.

My phone interrupts my thoughts.

"Hi, Sal, what's up?"

"I'm locating all the accounts for Ignazio and Gabriella so I can freeze her assets, or play with the amounts when you give me instructions. Francesca has alerts on the dark web should Ignazio hire any contract killers."

"It would be funny if she contracted Francesca by accident. That might be an idea," I suggest. "Excellent work. Ciao." I chuckle at the irony of Ignazio contracting our family's assassin. Why didn't I think of using Francesca as a plant to get close to her?

I wouldn't be human if I didn't think about the risks I take daily. Granted, life was somewhat normal, aside from a psychotic woman intruding on our lives. No large wars, well, if we take out the near-miss between Dante and Don Conti. What a shitshow that was. All things given; we were fortunate to get away with our lives, and without heavy losses.

And who could have seen Massimo being part of the family? The old man got around. Massimo is a prized addition to the family, and his connections with the Albanians will keep them in their territory. We can look the other way for an infraction here or there. I'm sure we'll have to include them in some government contracts at some point—the share the wealth to keep the peace mentality, and other bullshit babble called politics.

One never wants a Don to feel slighted. And no Don wants to be told he's not making headway as far as progress is concerned. There always has to be a larger picture because everyone wants to add to their bottom line. Who doesn't want more money?

I park at Dante's estate and check for the guards who aren't evident as I enter.

"Ciao, Riccardo," Dante greets me.

"Riccardo, come, eat," Juliet adds as she joins us in the foyer. The house is magnificent as usual. Perfect for the two of them.

"Sure." I kiss her on each cheek. She puts her arm around me as we walk to the large kitchen. I greet Rosario as she sets plates on the table along with a bowl of hard-boiled eggs, crisp toast, and small cups with saucers.

"Is it going to rain all day?" I ask.

"I hope not," Dante pours us each an espresso.

Juliet appears different. Not in a dramatic way, but she's glowing more than normal. If I didn't already know she was expecting I would have suspected as much.

I've never regretted not having children, recognizing the fact I'm past my prime. I'm wonder if I missed something now that I'm older and pondering the mysteries of life. Who will I grow old with? I scoff at the thought. I don't anticipate growing old, not with my lifestyle.

I sit in the wooden chair because Dante loves to eat in the kitchen, and it appears Juliet has maintained the status quo. She doesn't stand on formality until the holidays. I wonder where I will be for Christmas this year and hope Liat will be home. Maybe we can meet up at my sister's.

"So, what is the plan?" Dante helps himself to eggs which he cracks open, cuts, and covers with a drizzle of olive oil. He tosses back an espresso and pours another.

"Hm, well, I think we need to wait for the rest to show up. Everyone has an expertise. I'm concerned over my ward who is in St. Petersburg. Of all the places she could dance, she threw a fit to go, against my will," my voice gives away the one area I've been defeated. My weakness is Liat. It's hard to think of her grown-up. I'm bracing myself for the day she informs me she has a serious boyfriend.

Dante chuckles. "That ward of yours is as tough as a biscotti is hard."

He eyes me over his warm eggs as he grabs toast. I can't deny it's difficult to retain my stoic face void of emotion.

Or is it?

"She's a girl who's in over her head," I convey my

concern for her and the discord we suffered when she refused to listen to reason.

"What girl?" Juliet asks as she puts jam on her toast before taking a bite of eggs.

I send Dante a look that conveys, 'shut the fuck up.'

"Never mind, dear," Dante intercedes on my behalf.

"Oh." She sends me a quick glance and busies herself with another espresso, and two scoops of sugar from the bowl before dropping it in her cup and stirring it with the tiny spoon.

Swirling is how my head feels every time I speak to Liat.

Juliet knows her place and refrains from prying. She finishes her espresso in two sips, takes a few bites of food, and announces, "I'm heading into the office."

She kisses Dante's lips, whereby he holds her hand briefly before she slips away. She lightly taps my shoulder as she passes by, her way of including me in the family. It's the most physical contact I've had in a year outside of an occasional hookup with lonely women.

Dante has someone to share his secrets with for a change, I understand life changes. After Dante kidnapped Juliet, her biological father chased them, intent on killing them both. They deserve to be happy, she's a sweet girl even if her family tree has much to be desired.

I hear keys jingle, Rosario wishes her a good day at the door before it closes.

I'm not the ogre most would believe me to be. It's not that I'm totally opposed to a good woman by my side, no one is the right fit. It's not as if I give anyone enough time to know who I really am. Besides, I'm married to the Micheli family until my services aren't needed. I've never regretted a day with this family, and at times, it's easier to be with the men who break the rules than the ones who enforce them.

The death of my wife sent me on a dark path. Situations occur, whether it's internal pushback from the other families or our capos. It's how life works. If we make it home safely every night, I've done my job.

Dante takes care of me. I want for nothing. My house needs some work, but I lack the enthusiasm to change it. It's perfect for a bachelor. One day when I retire, I can update sinks and put in lavish walk-in showers, they appear to be the modern trend. Hell, we even have kitchens like the Americans with shiny steel appliances and pretty bathroom bowls instead of sinks.

"So, Liat is in St. Petersburg. She needs to get out now before we go in." Dante tells me what I already know.

"She refuses." I run my hand over my goatee and sigh. "That girl will be the death of me."

"Not likely. I think you are both stubborn." Dante finishes eating, wipes his mouth with a cloth napkin, and scoots his chair back to observe me.

I decide I could use a pick-me-up and help myself to another espresso.

"True. It's hard for me to tell her anything after letting her go to Paris. She has her headset on being a famous ballerina. I can't deny her that," my voice fades off in memory of her mother, a splendid ballet dancer.

"I know, but there are many places for her to be an understudy and other troupes she can dance with; why does it have to be this one?" Dante pushes his plate away, and Rosario dives in like a bird clutching a fish as she clears the table and cleans the kitchen before heading off to what I assume must be laundry.

"There are moves she can only learn there. The Russians do have a history with ballet." I raise my eyebrows, trying to justify Liat's decision. In her defense, maybe I'm overprotective.

"So, on to business." Dante stands, and I follow suit.

The front door swings open just then, and with all the fuss, it's like a circus. I must be getting old as it's like the Micheli home is filled with squawking ducklings. The brothers tease each other, and Francesca gets in a few barbs shaking out their umbrellas and putting them in the stand by the door.

I greet everyone as we adjourn to Dante's formal dining room, now dubbed the war room.

"I can't wait to get my hands on that bitch," Massimo states as he unrolls a large, laminated map of Europe.

"Is Valentina still working at the hospital?" The family is getting larger, and I have to keep up. Massimo has his own security, but there's nothing wrong with having too much information.

"Sure, sure, she loves it." He lays dry-erase markers on the table.

"Great, we need to find contacts who can get us medical supplies and some drugs like painkillers and a staple gun, you know, the things we need for this trip. It's going to take everything we have and then some to pull this off," I warn, bending over the table and circling the city of interest in black and yellow to highlight where we have contacts. That would be Sicily where Giovi reigns, and Massimo's grandfather in Albania.

"I'll get money. We'll need loads of it to pay off the contacts as we go," Sal volunteers.

"We need a team of elite men to go in through Belarus with our bag of goodies," Francesca adds with confidence. She loves tactical planning and physical confrontation. No doubt she's had her fill of caffeine today.

A pregnant pause fills the room. For a few seconds, it's the voice of any noise or movement. It's as if we all stopped breathing.

"What?" Francesca surveys the room where all eyes are on her.

"Honey, you have a way of taking control," Sal speaks softly.

"You like it in bed. What? I'm not good enough to venture into freezing tundra?" Her feathers are ruffled, but her bark is worse than her bite. It's the enemy who should be quaking.

Most mafia families wouldn't allow women to be involved in their business. She has her own mafia in southern Italy but hangs with us for Sal. It makes for easy transactions on deals between the two families.

"It's fine, we're just busting your chops. It's so rare to have such an accomplished specialist in our midst." Dante paves over the fact she's a woman doing a man's job, and she's never let us down. It worked to our benefit her drugs didn't kill Prende's father as planned. We had no idea anyone else wanted him dead, and that, in part, led us to where we are today.

"This is going to be an operation of dirty deals. We have no idea if our 'helpers' will sell us out. We're going in on shoestrings and bubble gum," I add. Under normal circumstances, this would be a funny line. But today, it hits home.

The room is somber; serious.

"My grandfather has connections here," Massimo adds, pointing to Belarus and a place along the border.

"Does he know who you are?" I ask out of curiosity as I circle the town he points to now covered in yellow.

"Nope, and I'm keeping it that way. It gives me the upper

hand and I can protect the Italian family business," he replies with a smile as if he's being chivalrous on a first date.

I respect the fact Massimo has the skills of our Don, Dante. Neither makes rash decisions based on emotions. With the possible exception being the women they love.

Still, he's a clever kid.

Dante's phone rings. He addresses Giovi before putting him on speaker and lays his phone in the middle of the table.

"I have connections through our cognac and gun channels with Russian Bratva. But I want to go. She killed my dad," Giovi makes his case.

"We haven't decided on the final team yet," I remind everyone.

"Well, I'm prepared to go."

"Look, Giovi, you don't have an heir; there will be no one to run your business if something happens to you. We need you to hold down the fort and work with a team here to help with support." Dante straightens in his chair and he runs a hand through his thick hair.

"I'll follow your wishes, but I'm here and willing to go," Giovi reiterates.

"Noted," Dante replies.

"Let's get down to business. First, I will fly into St. Petersburg, I have personal business there, and it's best if we don't all arrive at the same time. Francesca, do you have the passports?" It's important I reach Liat and make sure she's safe before we bring the war to the Bratva.

"Yes, they arrived yesterday."

I notice she's wearing Sal's engagement ring, and for a second, I yearn for a fraction of the love and commitment these men have found over the past year. It manifests in my chest, and I have no idea how to make it disappear, making it irritating as hell.

"We need Massimo to be with the men going in through Belarus; I'll fly in through Finland, Sal, and Francesca, you travel together after I've left. Marchello, I need you to work with Giovi to find us safe houses in Russia with his connections running cognac."

"I can do that. I can also secure guns there," Giovi chimes in earnestly.

"Great, I'd like Marchello to stay behind and run the business," I glance at Marchello who nods in agreement. "And Sal, you'll be our tactical man; make sure you get all the surveillance gear and then some." I nod to Francesca; she's an ace at everything. It's nice I can trust all the members of the family.

"I'm already on it. I've also ordered some items to keep us warm, and I'll get with everyone on what they need to be prepared for, the Russian spring, is only a word, because you guys will freeze your balls off. We don't want to lose them or get frostbite should we find ourselves in a compromising position."

"Okay, Francesca, you don't need to bring your sex life into it," Marchello teases.

She snickers. "Easy for you to say, Prende fell into your lap. The real Casanova is gone," she smirks.

"Gone from the public but very alive just the same," his quip comes just as Giovi has to ring off.

"Dante, I'll be in communication with you. Francesca, Sal." I look at them and catch them eyeing each other as if they will fuck at any minute. "Did you bring my encrypted satellite phone and computer?"

"Yes, it's by the door," Sal replies. I'm assured I won't be tracked while we're in a dangerous country and up to only bad deeds.

I turn to Dante. "Great. Make sure everyone is prepared. You're in good hands. Everyone has a skill set we can use. I'll see you next week in St. Petersburg."

"You going to be okay with that ward of yours?" Dante taunts me. He seems to find it entertaining how my ward gets under my skin. Knowing me the way he does and the fact I rarely share my personal life with anyone other than him, I assume he's amused.

I grimace, turning one side of my mouth up in thought. "Send me the information from Giovi; we need a few safe houses, so we'll be harder to find and it might split up their men who will no doubt find us at some point."

"Got it," Dante chuckles. "Don't do anything that would be construed as fun while you're there with that cute ward."

I shake my head. This younger generation has so much to learn.

4

———

LIAT

"Aleksandr, what are you doing after this season?"

"I don't know. I'd like to travel. Maybe we could do New York City together. It's only a matter of time before you land a spot there. Our teachers all think you have something special." He stops abruptly.

Ignoring his pause, I chew my food and try to read his face without him noticing. His face tells me everything I don't want to know. He's smitten with me.

We talk about dance and what to do after rehearsals this week, but I commit to nothing. Even though I feel perfectly safe with all the cameras and what I've been told are armed soldiers walking along the streets, he walks me home. Being from Italy, I'm used to seeing armed personnel guarding national monuments and statues.

My building is one of four, ten-story high-rises, with a courtyard in the middle. Most of the dancers share a flat. I was lucky to be one of only a handful of girls to get to enjoy the benefit of total privacy.

Aleksandr holds the door open as we enter the lobby of the building. The paint is peeling, and the elevator is broken, but it's warm and clean. We're young and fit, so walking up to the fifth flight of stairs is not an issue. I view it as a workout.

Aleksandr is sweet and reminds me of my 'cousins' in Italy who live with Aunt Vivian and Uncle Stephan. He waits while I unlock my door, and when I say goodbye, he bats his long eyelashes, and makes a joke, leaning in for a kiss.

I dodge his pass with my catlike reflexes and thank him for a nice evening before quickly slipping inside my flat with a quick good night. Leaning against the door, I wonder why I didn't let him kiss me.

It's not like I've never been kissed. I lived in Paris, the city of lovers. I had a few crushes until I learned the world was filled with men who don't know what they wanted. I can't waste time on men who are immature and fickle. I need someone I can respect, who is trustworthy and dependable.

Besides, I don't want to jeopardize my friendship with Aleksandr, my closest friend in the troupe. Have I done something to lead him on in some way? Between rehearsals and classes, we're around each other all the time. The forced proximity makes a romance almost inevitable. It's the same for movie stars working on a movie; they fall madly in love and get married. They later realize it was just an infatuation born out of availability. Love affairs which start on movie sets, typically end up on the editing floor.

I'm not one to open up with men. I've known Riccardo forever. He has an edge about him. He's different. There is a stillness about him I find calming. I'm creative, a bit wild, and seeking adventure in new countries, while he's a rock of strength and resolve. He's always in control, which tempers my irrational mood as it swings between euphoria when life is grand to the lows when life is a struggle. He gives me practical advice, and I take it. He's older and wiser than I can ever hope to be.

Kicking off my boots, I leave them by the door before hanging my coat on a wall hook. The first thing anyone notices in this room is the ballet barre running the length of one wall. It was left here by the last girl who lived here. I use it daily. To be the best, I practice as much as possible.

I'm excited Riccardo's finally coming to visit. I wish it was just to see me, but I get the impression something else is bringing him here. Over the years, I've learned what he doesn't say is just as important as what he says. I'm always trying to read between the lines and interpret his silence.

I was never told to call Riccardo 'uncle'. He's not my uncle. I don't consider him family even though he is part of the only family I have ever known. Maybe I remind him of my parents and his wife, and that's why he stays away for long periods of time, avoiding the painful memories.

His visits are always short. His private life is unknown. I'm not naïve in the sins of the flesh. He's still in great shape with a toned physique hot enough to make me drool. I can't help but fantasize about him. When my hormones need a physical release at night, I close my eyes, picture him naked, and service myself until I come.

I've overheard enough phone calls to think Riccardo is mixed up with the mafia. Over the years, he and Vivian whispered when they thought I was asleep, but I hear things. Information learned here and there over the years builds up to a larger puzzle piece.

I went online to research his past and surmised his bio has been scrubbed. He may as well be a ghost. The articles about the Micheli family are either old stories about the father's untimely death or new stories about their charity work and the millions they donate.

Nowadays, many mafia families are starting legitimate businesses to make money. I've watched enough Italian detective series to know they still operate their illegal operations behind the scenes.

My phone pings. It's Aleksandr letting me know he got home and had a great time. I text him back the same while I change into a cozy designer tracksuit. I didn't bring many clothes with me. The clothes I left in Italy are suitable for a Mediterranean climate, not an Arctic one.

I'm craving hot chocolate and paddle into the kitchen, pouring milk and a spoonful of powdered cocoa into my favorite mug. I pop it in the microwave and wonder how long Aleksandr has had a crush on me. We've always been overly friendly, it was fun, and comfortable while it lasted.

I curl up on the lumpy couch with my cocoa flipping on the TV, only to stare mindlessly at the screen because every channel is in Russian. I'm too lazy to pop a movie in the CD player.

My mind wanders to my parents, the few memories of them and of Israel is all I have. I wish I had more. I have pictures of them on my dresser. If my dad was alive, I wonder what he would think about me dating his friend who is so much older than me.

I feel lucky to have blocked the memories of my traumatic beginning. I'm not emotionally stunted like Riccardo. I remember Riccardo disappeared just after he left me with Aunt Vivian. I can understand a widower, a childless man, not wanting to be around a small child. It wasn't until a few years later I discovered Vivian is not my aunt by blood.

Riccardo is elusive, at times, withdrawn. It's as if he can't shake that day in Tel Aviv. I have no idea what it's like to lose a wife. I've never loved anyone enough to commit to a relationship. I hope I find my person. In my eyes, I already have.

I just need to make Riccardo see me for the mature woman I've become. I hope living in a foreign country might prove to him I'm independent and capable of taking care of myself.

The evening drags on. I lay in bed awake, thinking of the last time I saw him wondering how our meeting will go. I have no idea if he's seeing anyone. Aunt Vivian says he'll never get married.

~

IT'S OPENING NIGHT, and everyone is bustling around backstage like a hive of queen bees. The girls help each other apply makeup as opening night has to be perfect. I'm jittery. I'm not sure if it's stage fright or the anxiety I have waiting to see if Riccardo will show up.

Ballet has to be perfect. I have to be perfect.

When the curtain goes up, I'm Aurora. My performance will start with a seven-minute and forty-five seconds solo on pointe while I'm twirled around by four male dancers. You would think the lead role has the most dancing, but I have to be asleep like the fairytale for years. Then, Aleksandr kisses me, he's my prince, and we dance together in what I think is the most romantic story in ballet history.

Chloe screams, and we all freeze. She's fuming as she carries her phone. I suppress a smile. George, the prankster, has struck again.

"Who posted me eating a whole pizza?" she hollers and looks around.

We're quiet. Any girl who giggles gets her stink eye until they stop.

The director, Mr. Petrov, discreetly moves her backstage

and calms her down. After a minute, he claps his hands and tells us to go.

We hear the host make an announcement and line up.

I haven't heard from Riccardo. He will typically show up unannounced. In that respect, he takes his tactical training too far. But what do I know? Is it me, or does he hide from everyone?

The curtain goes up. The night has begun.

I dance to perfection. We trained for the shortened version. When we take our final bow, Aleksandr compliments my performance, saying we delivered a great show.

The audience gave a standing ovation resulting in two curtain calls. It was a magnificent performance.

Backstage, I chat with Aleksandr while covering my face in cold cream to take off the stage makeup. Hearing footsteps, I look in the mirror, and my heart skips a beat.

"Riccardo," comes out as a gasp as I stare at his reflection. Spinning around, I jump into his arms.

"Your performance was amazing," he says, releasing me from his bear hug and awkwardly handing me a bouquet of roses, "Here, these are for you."

His dark smoldering eyes feel like molten lava rocks and match the heat growing between my legs. It's now that I notice his beard is gone. If he looked good before, he looks even hotter now.

To avoid staring at him like a stalker, I bury my face in the roses, breathing in their sweetness. He's here, alone, away from Aunt Vivian's watchful eyes. Is it wrong to want him so badly?

5

______

RICCARDO

The theater is ancient, but it has been well-maintained, and the interior is stunning. We have ballet in Italy, but we never had talents like Baryshnikov and Nureyev. Maybe the Russians can teach Liat stuff no one else can.

Her performance tonight is the best I've ever seen, and the standing ovation reflects it. As the group takes their final bow, the male lead kisses her on both cheeks. His display of affection doesn't bother me. I've seen it before and it's normal. All eyes are on Liat, and she's clearly loving every minute of it. I wish her mother and father were here to see it.

Glancing up at the box seats, I'm surprised to see Ignazio and her lover, Vladislav Volkov. Ignazio is dangerous and unpredictable, so I need to get Liat out of here without telling her why. This is not going to be easy on a night when everyone wants a minute of her attention.

I wonder if Ignazio knows I'm here. I shaved my goatee to change my appearance, but she's too clever to be outflanked by a little manscaping.

I imagine she has access to Interpol because the Bratva controls every suburb and city. The Mayors and Governors are all connected, making it easier for the Sicilians to smuggle in liquor. I'm sure mafia's around the world work with each other in some capacity as we've become more akin to global conglomerates.

In this business, trust and loyalty are always a concern. Mafia in Italy, I know. In Russia, we have to rely on strangers. It's a dangerous trip. I'm nervous with good reason. Between the unknowns, and the foreign country ruled by communists, the penalty for what we're doing is catastrophic if we're caught with guns, drugs, or killing someone. We're guilty on all but one of those so far.

I use this information to strengthen my resolve to not get caught, and my reason for staying detached from life. I never want to put someone I love in harm's way. It's easier to avoid love. Even with Liat, I come and go without a schedule to keep her and my sister's family safe.

I'm used to structure and following the rules. Living by my rules, we all stay safe. If I'm to go down, I won't take anyone with me.

I watch as Ignazio and her man get up and leave the box. Who would have pegged them as lovers of classical ballet? Coming here may have been a mistake. If she identifies me before the others get here, nothing good will come of it.

We should have lured Ignazio back to Italy. Having her on home turf would have been a huge advantage. We discussed it, but Dante didn't want to use Juliet as bait with her being pregnant. Juliet is Ignazio's only weakness now that her father is gone. I don't blame Dante for being protective of his new wife. Having a baby was a luxury I never felt I could afford, and before I could reconsider, fate determined my childless future as I never fell in love again.

Blending in with the crowd, I make my way backstage. After being checked by one security guard, I'm allowed to enter. I walk toward a group of ballerinas stopping short of my princess.

Liat is sitting at the dressing table, chatting with her dance partner. He's young and handsome. Clearly, he only has eyes for her. I have no reason to be jealous, but my chest tightens. I'm sure it's heartburn from an early lunch.

I watch as she wipes the last inch of rouge off her face. Even without makeup, she's breathtaking. She is perched on a stool in front of a mirror, lined with bright bulbs, in her straight ballerina-like posture. She's a portrait, there is no need for an artist or watercolors. She is committed to my memory, her smooth skin, her bright smile, and her agile body perfectly hitting each mark to bring the story alive.

She's my opposite, like a sparkler, she is the embodiment of cheer, and happiness. For a moment, my load is lightened. She's a glass of water to a man dying of thirst. I'll never forget her as long as I live.

I'm a grown man in a quandary. With Ignazio so close, do I risk giving away my presence? I scan the room. Everyone here is with the ballet troupe. Liat would be hurt if she found out I was here and didn't stop to see her. Besides, what am I to do with the roses I'm holding?

Fuck, I'm breaking my own rule.

Straightening my tie and adjusting my belt, I put on my game face and approach. Liat hears the click of my dress shoes and looks up. That's my girl, intelligent and observant. Everyone here is barefoot or wearing ballet shoes. I'm the only one wearing shoes.

"Riccardo!" Her face lights up. She leaps out of her chair and into my arms. I'm taken off guard and at a loss for words as I breathe her in. Her rosy lips are close to mine. She kisses one cheek, then the other.

"Liat." I smile at her and hug her back.

This hug might be a mistake.

I can feel her lithe body through my suit jacket. She's pressed against me, and it brings up physical impulses I shouldn't be considering with someone so much younger than me.

Besides, her father was my best friend. Even though it's been fifteen years, I can't forget I was her guardian for ten of them.

She leans back and asks what happened to my goatee.

I chuckle, rubbing a hand over my chin. "Yes, I figured it was time. Besides, it can grow back." Suddenly, I remember the flowers. "These are for you," handing her a dozen red roses wrapped in pink paper. "Your performance was amazing."

She takes the roses and lifts them to her nose, inhaling deeply. She's still in her leotard, and her small breasts are flattened to the point of nonexistence. I've never been much of a boob guy. Her long legs and delicate features are more than makeup for her teacup size breasts.

Plus, there's always her personality to keep it interesting. Her bright smile is infectious, even for an old grump like me. Sometimes she gets sad, but it never lasts long. She definitely has a mind of her own. I attribute it to my sister allowing her to think for herself and me allowing her to venture out as I play the role of her guardian. I'm dedicated to being her safety net.

"If you have no plans with your friends, I have a late dinner reservation around the corner. I know you love Italian food."

Her dance partner introduces himself as I shake his hand. "You should go, Liat, you have the rest of the season to hang out with us," he suggests.

She nods, "Tell everyone I'll catch them the next time."

He nods and steps away, blending in with other dancers.

"I hope I'm not interrupting."

"Never," she quips, giving me an adoring smile. I'm stunned by her beauty. She turns me inside out. She's not a child anymore, that much is clear.

What the fuck is happening to me? How long has it been since we've been in the same room? Maybe Christmas two years ago?

WE WALK TO THE RESTAURANT, and the hostess seats us in the back per my request. The fewer people who see me, the better. The waiter brings us red wine and garlic knots.

"Thank you for coming," she sips the red wine and tears the bread with her fingers, eating like a bird.

"No need to thank me. It's not like I don't want to see you. I'm just always busy."

"How are Dante and the gang?" she asks.

"Fine, he got married, so now it's one more person to worry about."

"Security?"

"Yes," I reply without hesitation and drain half my glass. I'm happy I don't have to lie to her as much as I used to. She's astute enough to figure out I'm a man of wealth and connections.

"So, is this your first time here?"

"Yes, it's nicer than I thought. Very modern."

"Yeah, well, time does change. I'm grown up, you're here, and we're having dinner."

"We did this a few times in Paris," I remind her.

"Yes, but Aunt Vivian came along, too. This is just us."

"Your Aunt loves to shop. Paris is the place for that," I chuckle, remembering the bill for those shopping sprees. Is she hinting she wants me alone?

"I know. Still, I'm glad you're here. You sounded cryptic when you last called."

"Oh. Yes, I have so much on my mind. Let's talk about it at your place later."

"Sure," she murmurs, finishing her glass of wine. I pour her another. The waiter returns and takes our order.

"You sure you don't want to be out with your friends?" I ask in earnest. The last thing I want to do is disrupt her life.

Ignazio isn't hiding. She's savvy and plays a long chess game of cat and mouse. It's wishful thinking on my part to think we lulled her into a false sense of security. We only delayed the vendetta so Dante could return from his honeymoon and Massimo could marry Valentina. The timing sucks because it's still cold in Russia, but we can't let Ignazio regroup with her new lover and come at us again.

"Oh." She waves her small arm through the air. "No problem there. All foreigner's in the troupe live in the four buildings grouped together with a park in the center of the quad. Most of us see each other daily. The Russians, like Aleksandr and George, live nearby. Besides, I never get to see you."

Is she batting her long eyelashes at me? Her hazel eyes are greener than I remember. I lift my glass to sip more wine. I need another bottle. I drain my glass as my eyes check her out. Her complexion is flawless and seems to be perpetually tanned. Her body-hugging long-sleeve sweater dress shows off every curve and falls off her bare shoulders.

She's a woman. Her dark brown hair falls loosely over her shoulders. Some of her long bangs fall across her soft eyes as she peers through them to focus on me. Her hair was up for the performance.

She's sexy as hell, and she knows it.

Fuck.

Heads turned when we walked in tonight. It's rather busy here seeing as how it is late. I'm sure the eyes that took us in were looking at Liat. Her hips are slender, she's maybe a hundred pounds. Her tight ass is as firm as an apple under her tight dress. She knows the suede boots stretching over her knee make her look like a runway model. My cock twitches under the table just seeing her.

I call the waiter over to order more wine.

"So, what's new?" I casually ask, trying to distract myself and my cock which has a mind of it's own.

"Nothing. I hate the TV here. I'm glad you told me to bring my movies."

"How is my sister?"

"She's great. Your niece is debating her classes at college, and your nephew is still the annoying twerp, but he's managed to pass his classes even though he skips school all the time. He might even graduate high school next year."

I can't tell if she's being smug or pushing my buttons for not being closer to them. It hurt me, as much as them, to not visit more. But their safety is paramount to my wishes or desires.

"Nice recap." I tip my newly filled glass to her. Better to ride the fence here and see where this is heading. I can't tell if she's angry with me or just being cagey, knowing she can talk to me like this and get away with it.

She lifts her glass, "A toast, thank you for putting me through school. Seriously, I wouldn't be here without you."

"Salute," we both speak Italian.

"Here, it's vashe zdorov'ye."

"Right. Are you picking up the language?"

"Some. Bits and pieces. George is the guy who translates for us. He's nice, a bit of a ham," she shrugs her shoulders, gives me a cute grin, and takes another sip of wine.

"And Chloe?" I hold my breath, hoping the girl drama isn't like high school. My sister about had a heart attack at how mean teenage girls can be. I'm glad I was able to dodge most of it and only dealt with numerous distraught texts for days serving as an intermediary between Vivian and Liat.

"Behaving for now," she chuckles.

"What happened?" I sit straight in my chair to brace myself as the waiter swoops by and refills my glass from the second bottle he set on the table two minutes ago.

"Nothing, really. We just did a tiny prank. Nothing that will cause you strife. You can relax," she pats my hand. A simple gesture, but one of familiarity, and intimacy, like we've enjoyed many clandestine dinner dates. The affection she gives me strikes an unfamiliar chord in me. "Your face looks like you're going to implode. Seriously, it's fine," she scoffs.

"Alright. Just be careful. You're not in Italy," I warn.

"I know. I'm glad I came, but I can't wait to hit the next adventure."

"You're young. You have time," I reply from experience.

"I know."

Good, maybe she'll take my offer to go home later. Our food arrives, and we make small talk. Or is it small talk? She's young but savvy.

Fuck, now I'm worried she's here alone. I should have

put my foot down, but she's an adult who can go where she wants. She earns her money. I send her plenty on my own accord, once a month in a transfer, so I know she's taken care of, it's worth it to ease my mind.

Now, my mind isn't eased at all.

6

LIAT

inner was great. I made Riccardo squirm a bit by acting entitled. He wants me back in Italy, but I need one ballet season here, then I can go anywhere. No one gets ahead by quitting.

Even though Riccardo was always working and rarely around when I was growing up, it taught me good work ethics. I've learned from his example. I bet he's in St Petersburg for work, and it probably has something to do with organized crime.

I hope he stays off the radar while in Russia because the penalties for breaking the law can be severe, and forget about a fair trial. I wish I could ask him what he does to pay the bills, but we have an unspoken agreement not to talk about it.

Dinner ends and, he drives me home, parking behind my building where there are few streetlights. I feel as if it's intentional. He had us practically sitting in the kitchen at the restaurant, and now this.

We get out of the car and walk in unison towards the front of the building. The light dusting of snow on the sidewalk crunches under our feet. It's dark, late, and I'm getting colder by the second.

"Liat," he wraps his arm around my shoulders. "I need to say something while no one is around. I'm here on business and it might put you in danger. If anything bad were to happen to you, I couldn't live with myself, so I want you back home."

"Riccardo, I can't. I have a contract. If I break it, I might not get hired again. I've worked my entire life for this. You have the bills to prove it."

"I know. I know. How about you fake an injury?" I would laugh, but I realize he's serious. For him to ask me to lie, he must be involved in something terrible.

"What? No!" I want to break away, but he tightens his grip on my shoulder. I swear he could choke a bull with his bare hands. I don't want to cause a scene or draw attention to us. Someone might call the police. I can't predict the people here. Some don't want to get involved, and others report everything, living on their spy craft like it's their civic duty. Aleksandr tells me there are CCTV cameras hidden everywhere.

"Look. Can you take some time off? This won't take long. I just need a week to take care of something. Tell them your Aunt Vivian is not well, and you need to help out at home."

It's not unheard of and might work, but that's not the point.

"No, let's go in, it's getting cold." I want to end this conversation before he has a chance to talk me into something I don't want to do just because he's persuasive and intimidating.

"I have to return to my hotel." He walks me to the door and surprises me with a hug. That's a first. I've always been the one to initiate physical contact. "Think about what I said. I'll come around for breakfast. I'll bring food."

"Secret mission?" I ask quietly.

"Something like that." His look of concern has me worried. I've always felt safe around Riccardo, but my spidey senses are on edge tonight.

MORNING CAN'T GET HERE FAST ENOUGH. It's four o'clock, and I am still twisting and turning in my bed. My stomach is growling even though I ate that huge dinner. This feeling reminds me of my first solo. I had no clue my parents just perished in a car bomb. I assumed they were in the audience until Riccardo came to get me afterward.

I drift in and out of consciousness until six-thirty when I fling back the covers and spring to life. Riccardo is an early riser, so I need to get ready. I can rest later. I'm in the middle of tugging on my Lycra pants when the buzzer from downstairs makes me jump.

Shit. He's here at precisely seven. I forgot he used to be in the military.

"Morning. Come up." I pop back into my bedroom to throw on an oversized sweater and fluff my hair, letting it lay naturally on my back. I hope I'm mature and alluring in Riccardo's eyes.

I unlock the door leaving it cracked so he can walk in. The sun is bright today, filling the flat with light. A sunny day is always welcome, just like an old friend.

I fill the espresso machine and flip on the heat. This is definitely going to perk me up.

"Buongiorno," his deep silky voice is as smooth as olive oil.

"Buongiorno," I smile when I see his arms filled with groceries and immediately zip into action, helping him put everything in the kitchen.

"I thought you were bringing food."

"I have. This is food, fresh food. Not the stuff one boils in the bag, goes in a microwave or deep-fried like the crap kids eat today. We have the best food in Italy, yet the young people go to these fast-food conglomerates. And what the fuck is in something they call a handheld food anyway?"

"Oh, my." I roll my eyes. He glances over, thinking I'm looking at something on a higher kitchen shelf. He needs to stop judging me because I'm younger and I roll my eyes a lot.

"Riccardo, really?" I pull the bacon out of the brown bag as he produces orange juice, milk, and bread. "You think I don't have food? I can cook."

"One never knows these days. Your generation is all about your careers." He puts the juice and milk in the fridge before opening the oven to check for a skillet. "Ah, I see some things don't change."

"Old habits die hard," I tease, turning the nob on the small silver machine. "Espresso?" The machine hums.

"Sure, sure," he busies himself with the bacon, laying strips in the pan.

I chuckle to myself. He's so good at everything. Being a bachelor for so long, he knows how to take care of himself, but he's set in his ways.

"What?" He catches me studying him.

"Nothing," I place cups on the grate and watch the espresso drip. When it's ready, I hand him one. He briefly furrows his brows before downing his.

"What? It's not good enough?"

"Ah, well. Have you thought about our talk?"

I'm standing so close to him our shoulders briefly touch. His cologne wafts around me, a mixture of sea wind and springtime.

"I can go with you. You can be my bodyguard," I suggest flippantly

"What? No!"

"Relax, I was joking."

He puts the tongs down and looks me in the eye, "There is no room for jokes, not today," he says sternly.

"Okay." My eyes are wide, we've never had a serious disagreement, those are usually reserved for my aunt. I don't know why we give the women in our life the most grief, but we do. Riccardo is not to be played with, that much is certain. "Loosen up for heaven's sake," I jest, but I know this man may never give up his poker face.

I pull another skillet out of the oven and force Riccardo to move back from his precious bacon. It's taking all his attention. I grab three eggs, figuring he'll eat two, and grease the skillet with butter. I crack the eggs as Riccardo puts slices of bread in the empty oven and turns the broiler on. He's definitely used to roughing it.

The flat is small but it's even smaller today. His presence fills the room. He cooks with laser-like precision. He's a perfectionist. I know this because I'm one, too.

The air hangs between us in uncomfortable silence.

"I'm sorry I can't give you what you want." I go first because the silence is more awkward than talking. He knows this. He was a decorated army veteran in Israel.

"We'll work something out. Flip the eggs," he instructs.

I do so without testing them. He's a man one takes orders from, and I realize I've given up more control than I intended. Eggs are eggs, but I'm afraid it's a slippery slope that will start a pattern of giving in to him. And I'm not talking about leaving Russia. The sexual tension radiates between us even though he's not giving me an ounce of encouragement.

Fuck.

He returns to the oven with food on our plates, pulls the golden brown toast out of the oven, and drops a slice on my plate, two on his. He grabs the warm butter from the counter before sitting.

We're buttering our bread when I realize we need more espresso and I move as if to get up. "Sit, I'll do that," he says.

I remain seated letting him wait on me. I'm not a princess, but it's kinda nice having someone else make the coffee. Plus, I get to check out his ass while he has his back to me.

"Eat, your food will get cold."

He can be bossy, but I'm hungry, so I eat.

"Looks like we're at a stalemate. I'm not happy you don't trust me," he says.

"I do trust you. This is about me being independent and making my own decisions. I am an adult, after all."

His eyes devour me. My cheeks heat up as he stares at my breasts.

"Yes, you are a woman, I know your age very well," he murmurs.

"I'm sorry for the past, I can't change that. But you can't live your entire life in the shadows of sorrow."

"I'm trying to prevent the past from repeating itself. We didn't speak much about the incident. You were so young. . ."

"I know. But we're here. And this is now."

"Everything has changed, and yet, at the same time, nothing has changed." He props his elbows on the table, laces his fingers, and rests his chin on the back of his hands.

"You're speaking in riddles." I toy with my empty cup

and peek at him through my long eyelashes. His eye color is on the darker side of green than hazel. Why did I not notice this before? I thought they were brown like his hair before it started to turn gray. His beard was gray too, I like his face better without it. It makes him look younger. Not that I'm opposed to salt and pepper hair on a man in his forties, I find him distinguished-looking either way.

"I never found the person who planted the bomb. I heard a random name, but it all led to dead ends. This person might still be out there."

"We're not hurting anyone. Why would anyone hurt us?"

"Because they can. You assume everyone is like you. I see the worst in everyone and act accordingly. That's how I keep people safe."

"Dante."

"Yes, and now his wife. His family is my family, too."

"So where is he? You're here. You put work above me."

"I can't be compromised."

"I'm what compromises you?"

"I don't know. Relationships make life complicated."

"Uncomplicate it," I demand.

"It's not a good idea. This is the first time since a car and my life blew up, I can't see the final act. I don't know how my trip here will end. It's risky."

My heart sinks, knowing the weight of the past haunting him to this day. He's sacrificed so much for others. All he's asking is for me to ease his burden.

I wish I could lighten his load and say I'll go home. But it sounds like defeat to me, personally, and professionally.

"I'll think about it." He's asking a lot, and my heart grows heavy. Would it be so terrible to give him what he wants? I owe him that and more. He was able to turn my traumatic life into something normal. It's clear he has paid for it with his life, a life filled with survivor's guilt.

"Okay, for now, but that might change." His shoulders relax, and his face softens.

"Fine," I agree.

"Great," he counters.

I'm playing a game cashing in checks I don't have money to cover. What are the rules? Where are the boundaries? How far can I push him, and when will he give in to the undercurrents of my sexual awakening? He understands human nature. He reads people like I read the tabloids.

He's always been able to stay one step ahead of trouble. It's as if he can predict the future without a crystal ball. What does he predict for our future? Do we even have one?

7

RICCARDO

"**M**m, now that's settled." I stand picking up our plates and carrying them to the sink.

Liat follows me, drying the dishes after I wash them. Apartments here do not come with dishwashers or clothes dryers. Italy was the same when I was a kid, but now most places have modern amenities.

I hand Liat a plate, and our fingers touch, sending a jolt up my arm stronger than a double espresso. I'm cursed. How can this be? After my hard-on at dinner last night, I've been wrestling with what her father would think. It's just wrong on so many levels. Not only is she young enough to be my daughter, but she's also too good for me. I don't deserve her.

The touch causes a ripple in my universe. Time is suspended. All the pain in my heart disappears, similar to the sun burning off the morning fog. Her lips are the color of fresh strawberries and just as tempting. I cannot resist my desire to taste them. I know they will be warm and sweet.

Our fingers entwine, and the plate slips from my hand,

and crashes to the tiled floor, shattering into a million pieces. Neither of us cares.

I lose control and ravage her lush lips like I'm drowning, and she's my last breath. She returns my kiss, pushes against my lips, and grabs my biceps. I suck on her bottom lip pulling it into my mouth.

Adrenaline courses through my veins. I pull her into my chest. The warmth of her body against mine fills the numbing void I've lived with for so long. I relish being with someone who wants me, in spite of myself.

My cock is hard, I hope the zipper in these pants keeps the barn door closed. I run my hand down her leg and grab her ass, forcing her body into mine. She moans against my lips letting me know she wants this as much as I do.

Liat has never mentioned a serious boyfriend. I suspect she's a virgin. I shouldn't take this further, but the dam is now broken, and the floodwaters are carrying us away. It's too late to change amid the shifting tide. And even if I stopped now, I'd have painful blue balls for a week. I don't have that kind of time.

She manages to get my shirt unbuttoned, tossing it to the floor.

"You're too —," I start.

"Stop," she demands before nipping my bottom lip.

Fuck, I taste blood in my mouth. This fucking turns me on even more. Our eyes meet with mutual lust. I grab a fistful of her hair and give it a yank.

She winces and leans back, exposing her neck. I start at her earlobe and work my way down her graceful neck as I nip at it with my teeth. Shit, she'll have to cover the marks with makeup later.

We're shedding our clothing as we kiss, and before I know it, we're in her bedroom. With my belt gone, my trousers fall around my ankles. I step out of them and kick everything out of the way in a frenzy. I'm mad to have her and crazy if I don't.

She's naked and gorgeous, a vision I never could have imagined in a million years. Her cheeks, flush with desire, match the pink in her nipples. Her breasts are just as I imagined, petite and perky. She's too thin, but it doesn't slow me down. I will make her eat more.

I pick her up, and she squeals as I toss her on the bed. I catch a smile on her face when I join her. With one hand, I smooth her hair back, tracing the side of her face so I can commit this moment to memory for as long as I live.

"Have you been with anyone?" I need to know; I'd be jealous if she had another lover.

"No."

I want to be her first, and I'm relieved knowing no other man has touched her like this, and there is no one to erase. I'd rather she lose her virginity to me than to some young punk who doesn't know his way around a woman's body.

But what am I doing? She's too young to know what she wants. It's further complicated by the fact she's been my ward. She's off-limits even if she is grown and technically no longer my responsibility.

I've watched her dance for years, but seeing her lithe flexible body on stage made me horny as fuck last night. I hate myself for wanting her. Since when do I let my conscious get in the way of what I want? I brush past the deterrent that plagues me, a million reasons to not take her. She should go to someone younger, nicer, and in a reputable profession. Rational thinking doesn't stop me. Our chemistry cannot be denied.

Running my fingertips down her back, she rolls into me enough and I am able to reach her tight ass, and I promptly give it a playful slap. This takes her by surprise. I think she liked it because she grabbed the back of my neck to pull me toward her and I take the opportunity to suckle her breast. I'm slow and deliberate, playing with her nipples, both are super responsive. I nip one, then move to the other. I relish exploring every inch of her perfect body.

I slip my fingers between her powerful legs and push them into her wet pussy. She gasps with pleasure. With my other hand, I caress her abs as my fingers run over goosebumps signifying she's super excited. I push deeper inside her, slowly finger fucking her. I glance up to enjoy the pleasure written on her face as she closes her eyes and bites her lower lip. God, she's beautiful.

Her body twists under me as she wraps her legs around my arm, locking it in place. She's no longer an innocent child. She's a woman with desires. Her body is built for dancing and fucking.

I take her hardened nipple into my mouth, and my fingers work their magic until she moans, arching her back. I'm not going to be able to hold off much longer. I'm eager to pump my cock inside her as my balls swell with seed.

I don't want her to come this way, so I pull out, licking her sweetness off my fingers. Her eyes grow wide. I smile and push her legs further apart to allow me to enter her. My heart races, I have to be inside her. I would tear down walls with my bare hands to get to her. I'm a hardened criminal, and I've done much worse to get what I want.

"It will hurt at first, but I'll make sure you enjoy it," I whisper in her ear as I drop kisses on her neck and place my cock in the folds of her swollen lips.

Hovering over her, I rub my hard cock in her dripping pussy, making a few passes over her nub. She raises her hips wanting more, and my urge is to fuck her hard and fast. I've been trying to hold off, but I can't hold out any longer.

She tugs at my chest hair as I enter her. The more it hurts, the harder she tugs, and the harder she tugs, the more I like it. I remind myself to take it slow. She finishes with my chest when I no longer grimace at the sharp pain before moving her nails down my back as I push through her barrier in a quick thrust. She cries out in pain, clutching me tighter, her nails draw blood.

I welcome the pain as I sink deeper inside her tight walls. I want to pump her hard and fast, but I regain my composure, delaying my gratification.

She trembles between pain and pleasure. I give her a few beats to relax and get used to it. I move slowly in and out, breaking in a pussy no other man has ever known.

When she moans and grinds her hips into mine, I take this as a sign she likes it and plunges deeper, hitting different pleasure spots inside her silky walls. She's close to coming as her breathing quickens and her muscles squeeze my cock. I've never had my cock milked by a virgin.

Our eyes lock as her pussy quivers. I pick up the pace to push her over the edge. She climaxes, thrashing about under me as she clutches the bed sheets, ripping them from the bed.

Like a soldier jumping out of a plane, you have to know when to pull the ripcord. When I feel a tightening in my balls and a thumping in my ears, I let go, and waves of rapture rack my body. The release is an explosion of pleasure and pain I've kept bottled inside me.

The lack of blood flowing into my arms and legs render them useless. I collapse beside her. We lay there, catching our breath, our hands instinctively reaching for each other. No words are needed. I lace my fingers between hers.

When we've recovered, I wrap an arm around her. I rejoice when she cuddles up and lays her head on my chest. We drift into a quasi-sleep until I feel her hand on my cock. Her soft touch turns into a firm stroke, bringing my cock back to life.

She takes me in her mouth, moving slowly up and down my engorged cock. I love being inside her warm mouth but resist the temptation to come. Her lips make my head fuzzy with pleasure, I lay my hand on her head as it bobs, going deeper on me as she perfects her rhythm. Her tongue flicks over my cock, the intensity is too much, I pull out. Playtime is over.

"On your back," I demand as she complies. I take her hard and fast this time. It doesn't take long for her to come; she screams my name, and when I hear it, I can't get enough of her and move harder and faster. I come with a rush of euphoria, it's a long orgasm that leaves me spent.

I kiss her lips softly and our eyes briefly meet. Do I see love reflected in her eyes? Her innocence is gone, she's a woman. She turns on her side and slides her soft fingertips down the side of my face. I take her hand in mine and kiss her, emotions welling up in my chest making my breathing catch in my throat.

This isn't me. I'm the man with no ties, no commitments. And yet, I can't stop what I feel. I'm no schoolboy. In loving someone I'll create a weakness and I can't put her at risk again. Surely, this can't last. I have too many responsibilities. Am I risking her life? There's no way of knowing. She'll be safe in Italy soon. I need to clear my head.

~

IT'S GETTING LATE, and I have a laundry list of things to accomplish today. I need to get going and, I wait for her at the door. I never dreamed I would be here, fucking her like this. My instinct was to keep my hands off her. No doubt, the devil and I both flirt with danger.

I button my coat, "You definitely need to go home."

"Aww," she whines and purses her swollen lips into an adorable pout. There isn't enough makeup to hide the fact she's been freshly fucked. There is a glow on her face, not to mention bruises on her thighs. She's going to think of me every time she sits down today. If my cock feels raw from the friction, I know she's feeling it, too.

"Yes," I command, knowing full well she'll verbally defy my order. She's the only one who ever gets away with it, and she knows it.

"Let me finish the weekend performances. It's the least you can do," she implores me.

Fuck me. I had to go and dip my cock in her, but maybe she'll be more compliant. I can only hope.

"Fine." I shrug. "Just promise me you won't mention me or anything to anyone."

Maybe I'm getting soft in my forties. Perhaps it's being satiated by someone I really care about. She's my muse, the light to my darkness. Instinct told me to leave her alone, but I had to dip my dick in her. My subconscious mind knew to stay away from her after she graduated from high school. Is it the real reason I've stayed away for so long? I've denied myself a relationship for so many years I need time to adjust to what's transpired here today and prevent it from happening again.

"Fine, I only have Aleksandr and George to speak to anyway. The girls aren't very friendly."

"Keep your routine normal. Don't deviate. I want you on

a plane to Italy on a family emergency by Monday. Promise me."

"Oh, fine," she caves. Finally, I win! This is for the best, she'll be safe. I'm relieved. Mission accomplished.

She's the only woman I desire, and I need to keep her safe, too. I have enough on my plate as it is. It will be easier to focus on Ignazio if I don't have to worry about Liat.

Ignazio is connected with the powers who rule this city, but she can't remain hidden in plain sight forever. No one is untouchable. She's getting more unpredictable, and deadly by the day, which is enough motivation to end this vendetta.

The plan is to have Liat fly back to Italy the same day as the team arrives. Then, and only then, will I be able to relax.

At the door, I tell her, "Be good. Be careful. Don't slip up. I trust you to get home. Wait for me there."

I give her a goodbye kiss before she closes the door behind me. I hear the deadbolt click into place and smile.

Good girl.

8

———

LIAT

Finally, Riccardo sees me for me. The sex–incredible, and I can't wait for more. My skin still tingles from his touch. My pussy is sore from being stretched and pounded, but it's a good kind of sore. It's what I've fantasized about for years.

Sadly, I can't share my experience with anyone. I promised Riccardo I wouldn't. I'm the closest to Aleksandr, but because he has a crush on me, he would not be thrilled if I had sex with someone other than him. Men are jealous that way. It's like they don't want you until they know you have someone else interested in you.

The age difference will be an issue, especially with Aunt Vivian. I'm assuming people will find out eventually, but what if I'm his dirty little secret, and that's why he doesn't want me to tell anyone?

I text Riccardo. *Hope your hotel room is nice.*

It's not something I would normally text him, but normal left the train station a few hours ago. I've fallen into lust. I'm not sure how Riccardo feels. I've been told men change after sex. Girls in high school had issues with boys pulling away after intimacy with no explanation. Some were dumped or ghosted within hours of a hookup. It always seemed like the guys wanted it to be over, not the girls.

Hopefully, Riccardo is different. He's mature. Surely, he won't treat me like that. I've had the biggest crush on him since high school. I could tell he was reluctant to take it to the next level today, but our connection is undeniable. He's the one driving this bus, so it is on him if it was a mistake.

My phone dings.

Yes, fine. Remember your promise. I have to work. Book your flight now.

I'm used to being his ward. I'm not used to having a warden.

Fine.

Harrumph.

He texted. Granted, it was to check on me and treat me like a child, but he texted. This means it's not a one-time thing to him.

I book my flight like a dutiful ward, putting it on my credit card, so I don't drain my monthly allowance.

Before the performance, I use the barre to stretch. I'm doing what Riccardo told me to do and sticking to my normal routine. If I didn't, he would know. I'm not sure how, but he would know.

There was no discussion about what would come next. Men like Riccardo don't talk about their feelings. He's elusive and broody. That will never change. He's been this way for as long as I remember. I don't want to come off as insecure or immature. I have to play it cool and not be a bother to him.

I go through the motions of my day with a light lunch followed by a shower. As I put my hair up in a tight ballerina bun, I pump myself up for tonight's performance. I receive a text from Aleksandr asking if he could pick me up on his way to Mariinsky Theater.

I reply, sure, I'll meet you downstairs.

I step into my knee-high boots and button my winter jacket. It's cold outside, but not the bitter cold it was a month ago. The snow has melted, leaving behind a dirty slush.

"ALEKSANDR," I give him a hug as I settle into his passenger seat.

"What have you been up to today? You didn't answer my texts this morning," he asks as he pulls into traffic.

"Not much, I was feeling homesick, so I watched some movies in Italian. You?"

"Ha. You finally hooked it up?"

"Laptop. Yes," I lie. Everything hooked up to the TV registers a tracking device for all I know. It's the world we live in. With a cell phone, everyone is a beacon. No one can hide.

"Fine. What did you eat, candy or popcorn? When we go to the movies, you get a large soda and miss all the good parts because you're in the toilet peeing."

We laugh about it. I thank him for picking me up. He glances my way, and I wonder if it's written on my face or my neck. I covered my hickeys before leaving home. Did I miss one?

As soon as he parks, I get out, walk ahead of him into the building, and make an excuse to slip into the girl's bathroom.

I peer into the mirror. Fuck! There's a mark. I'll be sure to do my own makeup today just to ensure no one notices. I make my way backstage, weaving between dancers in different states of readiness, Chloe makes a beeline for me.

Shit. Shit. Shit.

"I heard you were hanging out with Aleksandr and George the day I ate pizza. You're like the three fucking stooges," she places her hands on her hips, and her lips curl into a snarl.

"We hang out all the time, they're my friends." I hang my coat and take my seat at the dressing table.

"What is on your neck?" she asks, making sure she's loud enough for everyone to hear. I grab the makeup powder and apply it to my face and neck.

Aleksandr saves me by asking her a question and changing the subject. He's probably figured out I was with someone because I always return his text when I'm not working.

We're alike in that regard. He hates living at home with his family, and I hate being alone. Neither of us has a social life, preferring each other's company over the company of others.

It's not easy to build bonds with people in this business when everyone has an agenda to claw their way to the top, no matter the cost. Most will stroke your ego with one hand while stabbing you in the back with the other.

I always thought since my mother danced, I could as well. But the world of ballet is a double-edged sword, and the trick is knowing which edge will cut you. To be successful, you watch your back and trust no one. Those who say it's lonely at the top know from experience.

In front of a sold-out audience, we pull off a flawless performance. Everyone is happy, and Aleksandr gives me a ride home. I wanted to ask him why he helped me earlier, but I decided against it. I might end up spilling the beans about popping my cherry. I'd prefer not to lie. I'm no good at it.

"Were you really watching movies earlier? It was a nice day. We usually meet for an espresso. I just want to know the truth." He takes his eyes off the road long enough to study me, and I wonder if he's been trained by the secret police. It never crossed my mind before now.

"I was home. I'm pretty much a homebody, you know that. I used the barre to practice and rested up for today's performance.

"Okay, can I walk you up?"

"I'm fine, really."

Besides, I'm dying to find out if Riccardo has texted me again and I can't risk it with him around. One never knows who to trust, especially here in Russia, where secrets permeate everything. Riccardo told me all this before I came, but I was so excited to get accepted I ignored his warnings. Now, I'm wondering if I should have come at all.

My gut instincts have served me well over the years, but I'm no savant. I'm not in Riccardo's league when it comes to reading a situation. Now, more than ever, I'm glad I listened to Riccardo's advice and booked my flight. Just two more days, and I'll be home under sunny skies. The thought of warm days and fresh pasta are making me homesick. Maybe it's time to find more like-minded people in other countries where the only politics I have to worry about are in my troupe.

9

———

RICCARDO

Fuck, I need a cigarette. I picked a bad time to finally end a lifetime of smoking. A smoke right now would help me feel better about last night. I'm the devil incarnate for deflowering Liat.

I should have resisted the temptation, but she went from a mousy teenager to a hot little number overnight. I couldn't say no. She made me come undone, she's my weakness now.

If her father were here, he would think I'm an ass and tell me to find someone my own age. I could always count on him to do the right thing, and he didn't deserve to die. I've lost a lot of friends in this business, but his death hit me particularly hard. Finding and killing Phantom won't bring Levi back, but it will help me sleep at night.

I go back to my hotel room to check out and mess up the bedsheets to make it look like I slept there. It's as if I'm back with the Israeli government doing a covert operation. Some habits never die.

I'm meeting with Giovi's contact, who's been paid to set us up with a safe house where we can stay and hide the weapons we're smuggling in shipments of cognac, euros, rubles, and dollars. We found out the President of Belarus is in bed with the Russian oligarchs, and they allow illegal activity across their border. It makes for a longer journey, but it's the best way for our soldiers to avoid detection.

The timing on this thing with Liat sucks. I'm here to work. I need to focus, and being with her definitely creates a distraction. One mistake and someone could die, or I could end up rotting in prison.

The genie is definitely out of the bottle. Too bad this genie is not here to grant me three wishes. No, this genie is here to complicate my life. This could go either way. Liat will be pissed at me for taking her V-card, especially if I fuck this up, or, she'll start picking out baby names. To be honest, I'm not sure which reaction I would prefer.

My phone pings, and it's a text from Dante. His plane will land soon. I notify him I'll be at the airport. He flew commercial to avoid drawing attention with a private jet. There's no way to get a gun past airport security, so he won't have a weapon until later. We plan to coordinate with the others so we can obtain information from our local contacts and firm up our final game plan.

We're trying the old divide-and-conquer strategy to stay off the radar. It's always worked before. While Dante is flying in, Francesca and Sal are on a train from Finland. Francesca made sure to infiltrate the Interpol database and change our pictures to avoid being picked up by cameras. CCTV and facial recognition are everywhere nowadays and something I need to get used to.

Sal calls. "What's up? Did you find anything?" I ask, cautiously optimistic because setbacks are to be expected. Even more so when we venture outside our territory.

"Yes, I found more money. Looks like Ignazio owns a few boutiques in Russia where a few rich oligarchs are running heroin and cocaine. I can empty her accounts and transfer the funds whenever you want."

"Perfect, her dirty money can finance this operation. I also think we need to set her up with her mafia king."

Drugs are the leading epidemic in most countries, and Russia's proximity to Afghanistan makes heroin a huge problem. There are a few rich oligarchs running the show, but everyone else is poor. Most Russians are poor, living with multiple families in an apartment building, sharing one kitchen and one bathroom. I miss Italy. I can't wait until this mission is over. I'm done with dangerous side trips to countries I don't give a fuck about. But Ignazio is my kill now, she kidnapped Liat. I'll kill her for hurting my woman.

Knowing we can steal Ignazio's money makes me happy. However, Liat makes me the happiest I've ever been. But don't all romances start that way? All rainbows, and fireworks in the beginning until the buzz wears off? The pessimist in me prevails, will Liat be any different? Then I kick myself for being so obtuse. I love her, I'm killing anyone if they so much as put a hand on her. We have a clean slate, If I can remain focused, there will be no more ghosts to plague us when I leave here...

"Wait, are you like—happy?" Sal asks, picking up on the change in my tone.

I never saw myself as someone deserving of happiness. Happiness was for other people, not me. Last night felt like the first warm sunny day after a long cold winter. Will there be more sunny days? I don't know. It's not in my nature to be optimistic.

"I'll be happy when we destroy Ignazio. When you move her money, make it look like she stole from her current lover. Vladislav Volkov is his name. He's a governor here in St. Petersburg. He's more powerful than our contacts, and that Russian is worth billions."

"Thankfully, we're using the Albanians entrenched in the underground, and the men from Belarus have no allegiance to anyone. In other words, they can all be bought," Sal points out.

Based on his confidence, I'm reassured we can pull this off. Mercenaries are useful to us even if all they care about is their payday.

"One more thing, I need you to ask Francesca to look on the dark web of hers for someone named Phantom."

"Does this Phantom have anything to do with Ignazio?"

"I don't think so. It's an old enemy I suspect is hiding in Russia. I figure since we're here, why not check it out? It was a long time ago, might not even be relevant."

"Fine. We'll be there tomorrow."

"How is Marchello doing with the business back home? Any issues?"

"No, he's quite capable. We've doubled the security on him, Juliet, Mama, Valentina, and Prende."

"Good." I rub my chin, missing my beard. I'm still getting used to it.

"I gotta run. I'll let you know where to meet us when you get here."

"Great. Ciao." I hang up and slide the phone into a pocket inside my jacket. This way, it's harder for someone to clone or steal it. These smartphones are great, but they're also a gateway to criminal activity and fraud.

I grab my bag on the way out. It's always packed and ready to go. I throw it into the back of my rental car and drive to a small café near the Fontanka River. Nevsky Prospect is a busy street, so I can blend in with the crowd.

I can't afford to let my guard down again. Yes, I slept with Liat. She wanted me. I could see it in her eyes. I'm not sure who kissed who, it happened so quickly. Lust will do that when it's been pent up too long. I'm no angel, God knows I was horny as fuck for her, but I should have stopped myself

Thinking of Liat, I text her.

"Did you book a flight?"

"Yes, stop worrying. I've got it covered."

"Great."

"I told you I would do it, and I did," followed by an angry face emoji.

I sense her attitude and shake my head. Young people nowadays. I'm not asking her to wear a burka and hide in a basement. What's with the attitude?

If we're gonna make this work, we need to redefine our relationship. How are we supposed to act now that we've crossed the line and broken all the rules? I have no idea what she expects from me. Disappointed by our limited time together, I can't wait to see her again. Does she still want to make it on Broadway? She's always dreamed of the New York City Ballet. I want all her dreams to come true. She'll have so many opportunities in her personal and professional life. I won't be surprised by her popularity and men flocking to her. I'm sure she'll outgrow me.

I arrive at the café and order a coffee using the few words of Russian I know. I pay with rubles, collect it, and find a booth near an older couple reading the national newspaper. Always best to sit next to people who are not paying attention.

A man half my age comes in and orders a coffee. He's wearing the requisite matching black leather jacket, Adidas track pants, and sneakers. With his choice in euro-fashion, he fits right in. As he passes by, a piece of paper drops on my lap. I palm it like a magician.

I wait for him to leave before I stand, I drop my coffee in the trash on my way out. Once I'm a safe distance away, I open the note. Written on the paper is an address. This must be the safe house we were promised. There are two. We need both. There's a small army on the way, all with guns and party favors that explode to make sure we're not outgunned. I don't assume anything and am always prepared for the worst-case scenario.

Sitting in my car once again, I pull my road map from the glove compartment having anticipated the possibility my phone is compromised. Who knows what they know of us here? That's why I hate to go to countries without more time to prepare.

The safe houses are on the outskirts of town in the middle of nowhere. The driveway is blocked by a solid metal gate, I hold my breath, hoping it's not a setup. This would be a perfect ambush if our friends double-crossed us. My fingers grip the steering wheel as I retain my stoic face and hope for the best as my heart beats in double time. When the gate opens, I breathe a sigh of relief hitting the gas pedal without hesitation.

Fuck, I didn't want to be in the field like this again, but I owe Dante. He saved my life. I'll do whatever it takes to save his growing family. I just hope we all make it out alive I surmise as I proceed cautiously and drive past a vast country house as two men stand guard at the dilapidated garage and motion for me to drive toward them.

The garage door is old and looks broken, but the men open it with a gadget in their hand. I pull in. I turn the car off and exit, the garage has concrete flooring, and it hits me, the run-down look is camouflage! I muffle my chuckle at their brilliance, and relief washes over me. It appears we're in good hands. For how long, I don't know.

I don't know much about how the Russian or Belarusian mafia work, but I'm sure we'll figure it out. The next step is to get everyone here, gather intel, and formulate a plan.

10

LIAT

Something has Riccardo spooked, and now I'm scared. Afraid of what, I don't know because he never tells me anything. Instead, he treats me as if I'm too fragile or too naïve to handle the truth.

It's no wonder he's never had a girlfriend. What woman is gonna put up with his macho attitude? His only friend is Dante. Clearly, he's haunted by the past, but he needs to embrace the future. He has spent enough time blaming himself for circumstances beyond his control.

As I pack a small carry-on bag for my trip home, the still air void of sound is a prelude to a horror flick right before the dramatic music starts. I pop a movie into my portable CD player for noise. In the event I don't come back, I take my parent's picture out of the frame and put it in my luggage. I better leave all my dance stuff here. I don't need ballet shoes and leotards if I'm going home to help my Auntie.

I love dancing, but I could use this break. I need some time to figure out what I want to do with my life. I can't dance forever. Dancers are no different than professional sports athletes; we can only take the physical demands on our bodies for so long before they give out. Physically I'm fine; this is more of a mental break.

Living in Russia has reshaped my views of what is necessary to be happy. I took so much for granted before I landed here. Seeing what little these people have, inspires me to focus more on the practical, and less on the material.

I used to worry about not wearing sexy stiletto heels because of my feet. Not anymore. My toes may be crooked and bruised, but no ballerina worth her salt has pretty feet. It's all part of the illusion known as ballet. Remove the cute tutu and tiara, and you'll find an ugly mess hidden beneath it all.

If my mother had lived, she would have warned me about training in Russia. But I have no regrets. I've learned so much, like how to make more dramatic turns and reach a higher extension, signature traits of Russian neoclassical ballet.

Dance here is deeply rooted in the culture. Initially, it was the children of the aristocracy who were taught ballet. Now, anyone can go to ballet school, but it's not summer camp. The instructors push harder and demand more than their American and French counterparts. They want the best, whatever it takes. By that, I mean they can be cruel physically, and mentally.

My phone rings. It's Aleksandr. He wants to pick me up for a late breakfast. To avoid looking suspicious, I agree to hang out with him. Plus, it will keep me from staring at my phone, waiting to hear from Riccardo.

I thought our tryst would make things change between us. The not knowing is driving me crazy. My mind comes up with all kinds of worst-case scenarios. If something happens to Riccardo, who will take care of me?

Sex with him was amazing, and I can't wait to learn more. Sex is exciting, and by all accounts, he's an attentive lover. He better not go back to treating me like a child after he's had me as a woman.

Aleksandr should be here any minute. He lives nearby in an apartment he shares with his parents, grandparents, and two younger brothers. I've never hung out at his place for long as he prefers mine or George's. I wonder why.

I barely have time to hide my luggage under the bed before he buzzes the intercom downstairs. I buzz him in and open my door.

"Aleksandr," I exclaim, faking my enthusiasm. The culture here isn't touchy-feely. No offense, the guys here are fun, just not hot-blooded, and affectionate like Italians. I blame the lack of warm vibes on centuries of having their head on a swivel and not knowing who to trust. When friends, neighbors, and even family members can rat you out to the KGB, you trust no one.

"Ah," Aleksandr exclaims as he walks in and notices my movie. "I see you're watching movies in Italian. How is the disc player working out?"

"Perfectly, can I get you tea or espresso?"

"No, I'm fine," he says, looking pleased to see evidence to support my story. I know he thought, I was lying about watching movies. I never suspected Aleksandr of spying on me. On the other hand, this world can be lonely. Why would anyone want to befriend me? Aleksandr and George were welcoming to me, and fun, so we're a good match.

I work so hard, my social life lives unattended. Should I be suspicious of Aleksandr? Is he here to make sure I'm not lying to him? Why is he so curious? Why is he interested in me when he's handsome and popular? He can have any girl he wants. There are prettier girls in the troupe. Surely, he's had a girlfriend.

"Do you want to grab something to eat before we head to the theater? We have a matinee today, so we have to eat now, or not at all."

"I'm fine." His eyes wander to the barre, "Have you been stretching?"

"Always. I refuse to give Chloe an edge. Let's not talk about work. Do you wanna watch this movie with me?"

"I thought we might talk for a bit," he says, running his finger over my disc player before turning to face me. "So, how is your friend?" His tone drips with accusation.

"Riccardo? He's fine."

"What is he here for?"

"I don't know. He's a bit of an enigma."

"Enigma?"

"Yes, someone that's hard to figure out. He dips in and out of my life, but he's always been there for me, like a Godfather." I stifle a giggle.

It's not far from the truth, but like Aleksandr, I must be careful what I say. We can't have the wrong person hearing and misinterpreting what I mean. Being a young foreigner is no excuse if I get into trouble.

"Oh, I see," he agrees and practices saying the word enigma.

"How do you do it? All these languages. I can barely keep French and Italian in my head. In fact, I'm losing my French accent."

"With so many tourists in St Petersburg, we hear different languages all the time," he replies with a shrug. I notice he's still wearing his winter coat.

"Do you want to sit? I'll take your coat. We can just hang here and finish this movie," I suggest.

My instincts tell me the less I'm seen in public, the better. Yes, I'll be on stage later, but I feel safer with all those eyes on me. When I'm alone, I'm nervous. The stage is my platform where I escape and become someone else.

"Sure." He slides out of his coat and hangs it on a hook by the door before he joins me on the couch. He takes off his fancy sneakers and puts his feet on the coffee table. It's odd, he's never had flashy clothing before.

"Nice shoes, are those new?" I eye his Nikes. Even though there are cheap, fake Nikes on the street, it's not worth it because they just fall apart. I can tell his are the real deal.

"Yes, my parents gave them to me on opening night. You got red roses from your friend, I got red Nikes from my parents." We laugh about it, and the tension between us evaporates.

I bet the money he makes from dancing is a way for his family to get a larger apartment. They've been wanting one for some time now. With so many people under one roof, things can get tense. He doesn't discuss it with me, I don't need to know Russian to understand the heated words when he and George talk about his home life when the the fact of the matter is I've picked up a few words. Call it instinct, I know something is not right at home.

The movie is Twister, and I catch him up on what he missed. The flying cow scene gets me every time. Alexandre worries about the cows, but I have to laugh.

Aleksandr says he never wants to go to America because it has tornadoes when the movie is over. I laugh and tell him New York City doesn't get tornadoes. That makes him feel better, and he promises to pick me up later.

"It's not a bad walk, really. You don't have to," I insist.

"I want to. Be there. . ."

He stops mid-sentence, and I wonder what he was about to say, but before I can ask, he's gone. I lock the door and head to the barre to warm up. One is only as good as the time they put into preparation and practice. It applies to a lot of things in life, not just dance.

I take my phone off mute and check for messages-nothing from Riccardo.

Shit.

He better not be playing hard-to-get. I slam my phone down in frustration. Maybe it's a good thing I'm leaving. If he wants radio silence, two can play this game.

11

RICCARDO

"You speak English?"

English is the international language of business, and business means money. Being out here in the middle of nowhere, I'm not counting on anyone speaking English, let alone Italian. Today must be my lucky day when he answers.

"Yes, but we do not use real names here, a layer of protection, you understand."

I understand fine and proceed to step out of the car as the two men with him eye me suspiciously.

"Only getting a small travel bag," I explain as I carefully retrieve my bag from the back seat. I hold it up for inspection.

A man with more belly than biceps steps forward takes the bag, rummages through it and hands it back without a word. He says nothing and makes no eye contact.

"Thanks." I take my bag and focus on the guy in charge.

"You don't know us. We work for a man in Belarus who's friends with your Albanian contact. He sent us here to house you and help you smuggle whatever you need across the border. Don't worry about the Russians at the border. We have them on the payroll."

I like his confidence. This must all be routine for him and his crew, just as I had hoped. We look each other in the eye, one mobster to another, and size each other up. I offer my hand as a gentleman's agreement.

"Richard. What do I call you?"

"John. I like Die Hard movies." He smiles and shakes my hand. He has the hand of a bricklayer, not a piano player. Judging from his missing teeth, he's had a rough life, and I wonder if they fell out naturally or got knocked out. Either way, I bet there was vodka involved.

"John, it is."

He nods and motions for me to follow him. The other guys stay behind to close the garage door so no one driving by can see my vehicle.

I notice his work boots leave an imprint in the thawing mud or is it cow shit, as we cross the yard. I don't know. I see my own shoes are trashed and silently curse Dante for sending me to this hell hole.

John is a large man, tall, walks like a cowboy in thick blue jeans, not the thin designer shit we wear in the city. This is farm country, so it comes as no surprise. Here I am in black slacks for lack of anything else. I didn't pack with the intention of digging ditches. I'll pay someone else to pick up a shovel if it comes to that.

Taking a closer look at John's camo hunting jacket I can't help but notice what looks like dried blood on his sleeve. I wonder if it's animal or human. Dante, what have you got me into? Darkness and heaviness exist here, chills run up my spine. I consider this a sign of bad luck. Only a black cat walking in front of me could be more chilling.

Once inside, I'm glad to feel the warmth of a roaring fire in the fireplace. Compared to the outside, the inside doesn't belong here. It looks newly refurbished, and you can tell they spent some money on the furnishings. In fact, it feels downright cozy with all the velvet couches, Persian rugs, and lace curtains.

He says the older woman in the kitchen is his grandmother. She waves and continues stirring something on the stove. Whatever it is, it smells good.

"Come," John beckons me down a hall to a bedroom I assume is for me. The window overlooks the back and what might be a pig farm. So, it wasn't cow shit. It was pig shit I stepped in.

The bed looks comfortable. I have my own private bathroom. Again, another contradiction. I thought we'd be roughing it in a shed and shitting in the woods. This country never ceases to surprise me.

These people have money, they just don't advertise it, which is perfectly logical. When people flaunt money, it draws the wrong kind of attention, especially in countries where most of the population doesn't have it. I'm sure the mafia is linked to the leader of the country, and no one wants to draw his rath. Better to lie low and blend in. I wonder how many of these men were in the military.

"Nice place, John." It feels weird using an alias, but it's just as well we keep things anonymous. Not like we're going to be pen pals after this.

I put my bag on the bed and follow him to the living room. His grandmother brings us a tray of hot tea and black bread. As soon as I get comfortable on the couch I remember to send my location to Dante.

"John, I need to text my partner telling him where we are. Is that okay?" One can't be too sure. It's always better to ask first than beg for forgiveness later. There must be a half dozen men outside with facial scars, neck tattoos, and menacing eyes. I want every one of them on my side.

"Sure, I trust you are not using Russian Sim cards?"

"No, it's a SIM card from Italy. We use special encryption, so it's difficult to hack." I text Dante the address and push send.

"I wish we had your technology. It's difficult to get a signal out here, let alone untraceable SIM cards," he mutters as he pours our tea.

I let him drink first. The tea smells good, but I would never take the first sip from a stranger in a foreign land. Especially one who knows we are carrying loads of cash to pay bribes and buy things on the black market.

This time we don't need to buy guns. We're bringing loads of weapons for ourselves and John's men. They probably have their own, but one can never have enough guns and ammo. We take a risk in arming them because one never truly knows whose side the other is on until the alliance is battle-tested.

I admit we're insane for thinking we can pull this off. But I tell myself if I die today, at least I got to be with an incredible woman before taking my last breath. Of course, I tell Liat none of this. She doesn't need to know how I feel. It's bad enough I risked bringing her into this mess. Being with her puts a target on her back, I can't be in denial that I might have inadvertently broken my own rules and put her in the middle. I'm hoping she's off the enemies grid. They will stop at nothing to get to us, so I can't relax until she's on a plane home.

Dante must not have been far away because our tea is still warm when he arrives. John's men bring Dante inside and I make the introductions.

"Ah, nice to meet you," Dante says while shaking John's hand. Dante puts his bag down and pulls out an expensive bottle of cognac.

"A gift to you, it has more friends on the way."

John's face lights up, and he motions to his grandmother to bring glasses. Even if it's only noon, I can't refuse.

"To new friends," Dante says, and we raise our glasses, "Salyut."

"This is rather tasty." Dante runs his tongue over his lips before he sets the glass down and takes a seat in the chair between John and me.

"Thank you. I trust the rest of the liquor has arrived. I have a waiting list for it," John sounds almost giddy over the profit he stands to make off our cargo.

"Oh, yes. It's coming in with other party favors," Dante replies with a devilish grin. Basically, these two Dons have immediately bonded over their passion for money and power. We're bringing John a prized commodity in exchange for his intel and safe houses.

John nods. "My men will guard the grounds. There is another house," he points through the large picture window. "That's for your use as well. I'm told there are five of you plus some other men." I can't tell if he's sizing us up for nefarious reasons or making sure we have the necessary accommodations.

"Yes, I take it you have barracks for the men?"

"Yes, better than that. We have a small farmhouse as well. It is yours."

"Thank you. We'll make sure your men get the delivery. The cryptocurrency has already been transferred to you."

"Thank you, Dante." He stands. "I've done my part for now. We have eyes and ears on the streets. You have my number should you need anything else. I'll text you her location when we have eyes on her. Vladislav Volkov's son Krill may be of help to you? Rumor has it he despises the woman you seek. Just remember Vlad is the boss of the contingency here in St. Petersburg, a powerful man to go up against."

"We don't want him, just Ignazio," Dante says, standing. I get up and stand next to him.

"Then proceed carefully."

I see the wheels turning in Dante's head. If Krill can be an asset, and we have a man on the inside, it could turn this suicide mission into a success.

We shake hands with John and thank him before he says goodbye to his grandmother and leaves.

"Nice guy," Dante surmises, sitting back down on the couch to await the arrival of the others.

"Very. I don't know about you, but this country has a vibe that gives me the creeps."

"I feel it too. Good thing we're not staying. Massimo is coming in with the contraband, and Sal and Francesca are on the train. We'll pick them up a few blocks from the station." I recap the plan to ensure we're all on the same page.

"Great. We can pull this off with a little luck," Dante says as he pulls two cigars out of his breast pocket.

"Yes, we can always use some luck." I take a cigar from him and pick up a lighter next to the ashtray. Does everyone in this country smoke?

"Where is your guard?" I quiz Dante.

"He's out making friends," he seems distracted, and I follow his line of sight out the window. He must be looking at the desolate farmland surrounding us, wondering how life brought him to this place of gray skies and leafless trees.

"Great." I lean back on the sofa, and puff my sweet cigar,

enjoying the sweetness of the caramel flavor on my tongue. This quiet will be short-lived. I may as well enjoy the lull before the storm.

"How did your reunion with your ward go?" Dante asks while stretching his long legs and puffing rings of smoke in the air. When I don't answer right away, he says, "I take from your silence, it was more than just a reunion. Did you defile that poor girl?"

The glint in his eye is one of approval, not distaste. Fuck, I can't hide anything from him.

"It's no secret Liat's had a crush on you since she was a teenager, following you around like a puppy. You'd be crazy to pass up that tight piece of ass." He rolls the cigar around in his mouth and smiles, probably picturing her naked. Then he pulls his legs in, sits up, and flicks his cigar ash into my teacup.

"Hey, no need to make it personal," I quip. "Christ, that's bad luck. I'm bad luck. I hope she'll forgive me for dragging her out of Russia. She flies home tomorrow. It's for her own good and my sanity."

"What? You've got feelings for her? Never have I ever..."

"Don't jinx it. It's better this way. We don't know Ignazio's capabilities. We're on her turf now. She's ruthless, and I can't have Liat caught in the crossfire. I've kept her safe this long...."

"I know, Riccardo. She's grown into a lovely woman. There's nothing wrong with wanting more out of life. You've done more time punishing yourself over the past than you have to live in the present."

"It's the way it is." I shrug in resignation. "I'm gonna go see what Gramma's cooking. Why don't you pick out a room? There are plenty of bedrooms down the hall."

"Good idea. I need to get in touch with Giovi and

Marchello and ask about the family's candy store," he stomps out his spent cigar in an empty teacup on the coffee table before disappearing down the hallway with his overnight bag.

12

LIAT

I can't believe I let Riccardo talk me into leaving Russia. What could he be into that puts me at risk? This is nothing new. Before I lived with his sister, we moved every six months. He made sure my schedule was never the same. I always arrived at dance at different times, and we never took the same route. He insisted on going inside first and looking for 'bad people' before I was allowed to enter. Even in our home, he was constantly on alert and looking for listening devices. So yeah, he's always been overprotective.

Back then, I thought he was just being paranoid, and I debated if he was stable enough to operate in the real world. Whatever cloak and dagger shit he was mixed up in with my parents got them killed. So, I believe him when he says he wants to keep me safe. He's noble.

Don't get me wrong, I'm grateful he cares so much, but at the same time, I'm frustrated because he never takes my wishes into account. I've been the dutiful ward, always following his orders even if I'm mad enough to scream.

Right now, I'm seething inside because I haven't heard a word from him, and I have no idea if he's okay.

I've decided, if he's not in touch within the week, I'll ask my aunt to call Dante. Whatever demons lurk inside Riccardo, they are not going away.

As promised, Aleksandr picks me up on his way to the matinee performance. My mind is elsewhere. I ask him to repeat what he's saying more than once.

"I'm sorry, just a bit nervous." I do my best to give him a reassuring smile because he can read me like a neon billboard.

"You're never nervous. Is everything okay?" He takes his eyes off the road to look at me.

"Oh yes. I'm fine," I try to sound convincing. Inside, I'm a wreck thinking the man who took my virginity is ghosting me, just like the other girls I've known. I guess I made it too easy for him. I should have played hard to get. I can't go back in time, it's too late to change my mind now.

Aleksandr drops the subject, making light conversation as we walk into the building. Chloe is being a diva in the dressing room, and I don't even mind because it means everything is as it should be. I miss Riccardo. He's always been on my mind. I've fantasized about him for years. I'm anxious about the next step. I want to be his girlfriend, and I hope he won't put obstacles in the way. He's never been one to allow himself to be pinned down.

If nothing changes in the next few hours, I should be fine. Aleksandr will give me a ride home. I'll grab my bag, take the train to the airport, and fly out tonight as promised. Regardless of what's going on with Riccardo, my word is my word. That will never change.

The curtain rises. The music starts, and Aleksandr is still on his phone. It's a big no-no, and I catch sight of the director, he's getting annoyed. Aleksandr sees it and hands his phone to a stagehand.

My stomach is full of butterflies and backflips as I wait for my cue. I tell myself the queasy feeling is nerves as I push Riccardo to the back of my mind.

The music swells, and Aleksandr makes his entrance with a series of leaps that defy gravity. Then it's my turn, I pirouette across the stage and into his arms. We become symbiotic.

I love becoming a different person on stage. It's another version, a better version, of myself, and there's no room for anyone or anything in my head. In a world that's constantly changing, the stage is familiar ground and keeps me grounded.

During the intermission, I give Aleksandr a kiss on the cheek and a hug.

"What's that for?" he asks and appears to be distracted.

"You're the best, you are an incredible dancer, and I hope you come with me to New York. Maybe, we can be roommates and go to auditions together," I say to cheer him up. He's a great-looking guy, just not my type.

Riccardo is my type. The dark, brooding type who says little and does even less to make me feel wanted. What would it take for him to text? Okay, maybe that's not how his generation communicates. So then call me. People have been calling each other since Alexander Graham Bell invented the telephone.

"For sure, Liat," his voice is forced, but his eyes remain friendly.

I wonder if something happened at home. Lately, I've overheard him tell George about his dad's drinking and gambling problem and how his parents argue a lot.

Maybe his home life is why he chose ballet. The discipline involved gives him the structure he lacks at home. Plus, it's a great way to escape the chaos of a toxic environment. He's always saying he wants his own apartment. A successful career in ballet is his only road to a better life and the independence he craves.

Ballet in Russia is not what it used to be. Some of their best dancers defected to the West, and never fully recovered. They continue to lose dancers to other countries where they have more opportunities and a better standard of living. Every time one leaves, it's a blow to the country and their politics. No doubt, when I leave, they will accuse me of the same self-interest.

Suddenly my stomach is in my throat. I run to the bathroom.

I lock myself in a stall and dry heave into the toilet. This isn't good, and it's never happened to me before. Usually, when I hear puking in the bathroom, it's a ballerina vomiting up lunch as a means to stay skinny.

The lights blink, signaling the end of intermission.

Fuck, fuck, and fuck.

I feel like I'm suffocating and gulping air like a fish out of water. From seeing others go through it over the years, I know I'm in the middle of a full-on panic attack. What is only a minute, feels more like an eternity as I put my head between my knees and focus on my breathing.

I need to get back on stage. Aleksandr and everyone else is waiting for me. There is so much pressure to finish the performance. The success of the show depends on Aleksandr and me. Quitting is not an option. Chloe would be more than happy to step in as the understudy. She can do that after I'm gone. Until then, I need to prove to myself and everyone else that I can do this.

Splashing water on my face is out of the question with

all this stage makeup. I wash my hands and think of what Riccardo would do. He would power through this. With that in mind, I stand up straight, inhale deeply, exhale slowly, and tell my reflection in the mirror to get it together

As soon as I leave the bathroom, I look for Aleksandr, and he's pacing backstage, waiting for me. His friendly eyes narrow when I walk toward him.

"The intermission is almost over. We were looking for you. Where were you?"

"Peeing." I fib.

"Are you doing this or what?" His tone is clipped and on edge. Funny, I'm in the same head space. We're so much alike, a relationship with him would never work. I see him as a friend, not a lover, and one of these days, I need to tell him. But not right now.

"Yes, let's do this," I declare, forcing a smile.

By some miracle, we make it through the second half without the audience knowing there is tension between us. In fact, they like it so much that we receive a standing ovation.

Later, when we're hanging out in the dressing room, I hug Aleksandr and apologize for not letting him know where I was.

"It's nothing. Forget it."

He still sounds annoyed.

"I'm sorry. What more can I do?" I plead with him.

"Nothing," he shrugs, "let me give you a ride home. Meet me at the car when you are done."

"Okay."

I have half a mind to walk home, but it's dark, cold, and too dangerous. I need to think about distancing myself from Aleksandr. He's getting too attached, even possessive, without a reason to be acting this way. His personal interest in me is affecting his demeanor.

I find him in his car and slip into the passenger seat while he starts the engine. Without saying a word, I put my head back and shut my eyes for the ride home. When it's taking too long, I look around and see buildings I do not recognize.

"Where are you going?" I ask while trying not to panic.

"It's a surprise." He stares straight ahead, refusing to look my way. This can't be good. I need to go home. I have a plane to catch.

He pulls into a dimly lit parking garage and stops. My door flies open, and I'm yanked out by two men wearing fur hats and black jackets with some sort of strange insignia. My screams are muffled by a cloth held over my face, and my last thoughts are of his betrayal, and I remember Riccardo's face when we said goodbye. After that, everything goes dark.

13

RICCARDO

It's dark as I drive down the designated street to pick up Sal and Francesca. If I wasn't used to seeing Sal so frequently, I might not have recognized him. Sal wears a winter ski cap and a long wool black coat. Funny to see him dressed for the climate instead of the cover of a fashion magazine.

I check my surroundings before I pull into a parking spot and wait for them to find me. Not many people are out. There are a few people walking dogs, and some young adults look dressed for the clubs. No one is paying attention to our coming and going.

The trunk opens, two bags get thrown in, and I hear the familiar thump of it closing. The side door opens, and Francesca slides in wearing a dark wig cut into a cute bob. Sal slides onto the front seat.

"Ciao, Riccardo," he exclaims. "It's so fucking cold. My God, I thought Finland was cold. Thankfully, this is a once-in-a-lifetime trip," he rubs his gloved hands together as if he's starting a campfire.

I turn the heater up. "Ciao, Francesca," I peer into the rearview mirror to catch a view of her, some habits die hard, "How are you?"

"Ready to get this shitshow over with. Did Massimo arrive yet?"

"He should roll in sometime tonight."

"Are we still off the grid?"

"As far as I know. I'll need you to set up our surveillance. We have word the Pakhan's son hates Ignazio, so we need to locate him and work that angle. He can be our eyes and ears on the inside."

"Excellent," Francesca exclaims. "Can we trust the source?"

"As much as we can trust anyone. We're not in a position to question loyalty without our hands being cut off."

"Point taken," she acquiesces.

"The Russian Pakhan is also the Governor here." I deliver the bad news.

"Shit," Sal replies, agitated. I can't be sure if it's the cold that's biting at him or the serial killer we're hunting.

"It's how these dictatorships run, baby. Don't stress. We've got a good team. I want that bitch dead. We can't get married with a psycho after the family," Francesca reaffirms our mission. She's always on point.

"Yes, you two have yet to set the date," I add, changing the subject as I put my directional signal on to enter traffic.

Living in Russia is like living under a microscope. None of us can risk an infraction and end up in prison. The Governor runs the city, and Ignazio has his protection. This is one reason I'm happy we don't have to rely on Russians— yet. Let the Belarusian men handle it. There's no need to announce we're here. Ignazio is a skilled killer who thinks ten steps ahead. We've been behind the curve.

We have no guarantee she hasn't set a larger trap for us. On the other hand, maybe she thinks she's safe. One's superiority over others for so many years can breed complacency. I can only hope she's gotten sloppy and lives with a false sense of security. Another reason it was prudent to wait over a month to seek her out.

I look at my watch, Liat should be on the plane by now. She didn't text, I messed up. I should have never touched her. My life is one of solitude, so why do I see her face like a vision ten times a day? My fingers pause over the keys of my phone as I hold back. It's a slippery slope. One text will lead to more, and then it's a relationship. Not to mention, others will think I'm crazy for assuming a woman as accomplished and beautiful as her would ever fall for me. She's like cocaine, addicting and pure. I defiled her, and I beat myself up over taking her virginity.

"Where are you taking us?" Sal asks while looking out the window at the bleak countryside.

"Farm outside the city. The house is nothing on the outside but rather nice on the inside. It definitely has more than just indoor plumbing and running water." I turn onto a highway and follow it out of the city.

"And. . ." Francesca leans forward to catch more heat from the front vents and peers over my shoulder.

"It's rather plush considering its location. I was stunned," I reply without enthusiasm and glance at my watch again.

"What's going on?"

Damn Francesca, she's so God damn observant. I can't get anything past her. No one can, which is why she's so valuable to us.

"If you must know, for many years, I've been responsible for a ward who is here as a ballet dancer, actually, a headliner. After her parents were killed, she was raised by my sister in Italy, and she's Israeli. I flew in early to get her out of Russia."

"Right, how'd that work out?" she snickers.

"Not well. I would have had better success if you talked to her woman to woman," I shrug and floor the gas, but keep it within limits in case they use drones or cameras to ticket speeders.

"That sounds sexist," Sal comments.

"Oh, you have a better idea?" My voice raises, taking them both by surprise.

"Hey, Riccardo, I'm on your side. We all want the girl safe. Did she leave?" Sal turns into the compassionate family member he is given our lifestyle.

"She should have texted me she is on the tarmac."

"I'll check things out as soon as we establish our own satellite Wi-Fi. No need to use the local network. I'm sure they have hacking devices we haven't dreamed of here." She pats my shoulder as if to reassure me. What the fuck is up with that? I'm the pillar of calm, but her hand is comforting. No one is overly warm to me because I have my wall up, and they are higher than the ones in Berlin during the Cold War.

The safe house comes into view and my heart races. I'm relieved, having arrived without incident, I finally pull into the garage.

We pop out like it's a fire drill and walk into the house like we own it. Dante stands and greets his family with a warmth I've never been able to muster. It's nice to see him in his newly found wedded bliss.

I hope Ignazio won't shit all over it. We're here to ensure Juliet's safety as much as our own. But Ignazio is a beast and cunning. Even though she hasn't been here very long, we're on her turf. We don't have connections with Interpol, but I bet her boyfriend, the Governor, does. I'm told Russia violates all kinds of rules in the international community just like they violate their own laws to suit themselves.

"We'll all stay here tonight, there are rooms this way," Dante points to the hallway, "and at the other end of the house. We have a second house as well, and I suggest we let our top lieutenants stay there. The rest of the men can stay in the third location. Has anyone heard from Massimo?"

Sal pulls a phone out of his right coat pocket. "It just vibrated. He'll be here in an hour. He delivered the cognac and is bringing the guns and party favors," he grins knowingly. If we weren't in a foreign land for nefarious reasons, the two would be out partying with the locals.

They might have different mothers but it's downright scary how much Massimo is like Sal and Marchello. It's crazy, but the long-lost half-sibling did bring the brothers together. As it turned out, Dante's mom knew all along her husband was cheating, so his grown love child was not a big surprise. The men complement each other in business, which is why the Micheli name has withstood the test of time.

I'm grateful Massimo has Albanian contacts in Belarus through his grandfather, not that I trust his grandfather. The old man is always looking for a means to get more out of a deal. He has left us alone since we gave him the little black book he needed after the murder of Argon. Let's hope he remembers we're not his enemy.

It's unclear if Massimo owes him for connecting us with his contacts and the smuggling route he has into this country. His grandfather is into human trafficking, which we refuse to be a part of. Francesca's family was involved with that business, too, and she took out her own brothers to eliminate their threat. We never want to sully our business with anything unsavory like that. There are some boundaries the Michelis' won't cross even in our illicit world.

I can't help but remember the Don in the movie Godfather was taken out after he refused to get involved with trafficking drugs. I wonder how long it will be before someone challenges us on our moral high ground.

"So, when is Massimo arriving?"

"Later tonight. I'll help him get settled, and we'll unload the gear."

"Great. Are you guys hungry? The house was stocked with food for our visit," heading to the kitchen, I caught a glimpse of Francesca handing antennas to Sal. He slips out the back door. She's so efficient it's scary. We'll have our own internet and surveillance up and running in no time.

Dante heads my way with coffee in his hand. "Is Liat safe?"

"I don't know," my voice quivers with worry. "I haven't heard from her. I texted her earlier, and nothing."

"Call, see if she picks up. You have to know." He turns to Francesca. "Can you see if the flight from St. Petersburg to Florence has left?"

"Sure. One second."

Francesca's nails make a click-click sound as they fly over the keys. She looks at us, "It took off an hour ago. Is everything okay? What am I missing?"

"I'm not sure. The passenger manifest is not available to the public, so there's no way to know if she boarded," I state as I push a button and it rings Liat.

The call goes to voicemail. Either she has her phone on

airplane mode, or something has gone wrong, and I start to panic. I tell myself I'm being paranoid. Liat would never lie to me.

Has she changed? Or is she missing?

I can't rest until I find out.

14

LIAT

I have a pounding headache and a chemical smell in my nose, and I gag. It reminds me of chlorine or bleach, and I breathe through my mouth to avoid dry heaving. Every inch of my body feels like a herd of elephants has run over me. Afraid to know where I've ended up, I open one eye at a time.

The first thing I see is the dim yellow glow of a bare bulb dangling from the ceiling. I wish Riccardo were here. How long will it take for him to know I've been taken? I'm still wearing my coat which is good because there's a chill creeping into my bones from the cold concrete floor. My teeth chatter as I attempt to pull myself upright.

That's when I realize my wrists are handcuffed. Shit. Not what I wanted to find. I check my ankles and see them in metal cuffs with a chain. I lean forward on my hands to get my feet under me so I can crouch and move into a sitting position.

The metal chains scrape over the cracked concrete making a chilling sound that reminds me of one of those scary movies when the ghost is heard dragging their chains.

I suddenly feel lightheaded and will myself to remain conscious.

Even though the light doesn't reach the corners, I can tell I'm alone. This is good, but I need to figure out how to get out of here before someone comes back. Whoever left me here chained like a wild animal is not someone I want to meet.

My mind goes back to Aleksandr. He must be involved. Hell, he drove me to the place where I was taken. Plus, he's been acting weird ever since Riccardo showed up. It's like he's a whole different person. What made him change, and why did he betray me?

Riccardo always says one can never have too much information. That's rich coming from a man with so many secrets. And where the hell is he when I need him the most? Who am I kidding? If he can't be bothered to text or call, what makes me think he's going to rescue me anytime soon?

I need to figure my own way out of this mess. It's a struggle, but I manage to scoot across the floor to where I can sit with my back against the wall.

I know my phone won't be here, but I check my pockets anyway. As ridiculous as it sounds, it helps to focus on solutions and not let dark thoughts take over. It will do me no good to have another panic attack.

Why am I here? Is this a human trafficking thing? If it were, I'd probably be with other girls and in another country by now. Am I in another country?

As my eyes adjust to the dim light, I see the room is smaller than I imagined, so small, a tall man would have to duck to get through. The place has a musty odor, I guess this is a cellar or bunker. It's cold but not cold enough to worry about freezing to death.

There's a white porcelain pot in the corner, and I assume

it's my toilet. Pushing myself up the wall, I manage to stand and shuffle to the pot. I squat and pee as quickly as possible in case someone is coming.

I shuffle back to my corner. Its familiarity gives me comfort. Looking for a way to escape, I survey the room again. This time I noticed one wall looks much darker than the others. I look closer and what I see makes me dry-heave. It's dark red, almost black, with clumps looking like tripe. The wall is covered in dried blood. I gag again as a wave of bile rises in my throat.

How long before my blood is on the wall? What role, if any, does Riccardo play in this? It can't be just a coincidence I'm here only days after Riccardo comes to Russia. Maybe he has powerful enemies. Surely, he would have warned me.

Could this be Chloe's work? She's rich with the family penthouse overlooking Champ-de-Mars Park in Paris. Maybe the family paid someone to abduct me so she could have my spot as a prima ballerina. No way. She's a diva, not a thug.

Which leaves only my best friend, Aleksandr. What does he have to gain? Money? He could use the money to get away from his parents or escape to the Western world and live the life he's always wanted.

Riccardo told me this country is different. I couldn't agree more. Is it too late for me to be rescued? The first twenty-four hours are critical. I know this from America's Crime shows broadcasted in Italy. I used to love them. I never dreamed I would need to know this information to save my own life.

I run the last car ride through my mind. I was so trusting. I never looked behind us to see if we were being followed. I'm not like Riccardo, who worries incessantly. I've learned the hard way people don't always show their true colors. Like a press release, they sugarcoat the truth.

When Aleksandr is dancing, he's happy doing what he loves. Who is he when he's not dancing? I've fallen into the trap of perception being a reality. I never bothered to scratch below the surface or got involved in his problems. Did I let him down? He wanted so badly to go to New York with me. It's all we ever talked about.

The darkness in the room makes me sleepy. Or maybe the drug is still in my system. If I sleep, it will pass the time and help me avoid facing my reality. I close my eyes and drift in and out until I hear the door creak.

My eyes fly open. Two large men wearing fur hats, storm in, startling me. I don't recognize their uniform. I take a mental snapshot. Will I remember it? I'm not sure, but, I want their balls on a kebab if I get out of here.

One of them approaches me, running his hand down the side of my face, from my cheek to my neck. His nails are long and filthy. His face is harsh, he has mean eyes.

They speak Russian, and I hear the word for 'water' as he pulls a thermos from his coat pocket. He takes the lid off and uses it as a cup to hold the water as he pours. When he offers it to me, I'm thirsty but shake my head. No way am I drinking that.

"It's good. Drink," he demands in English with a heavy accent.

I shake my head again, knowing I should hydrate but not trusting either of them.

The man sips from the cup.

Ah, this changes things.

I hold my hands out and take the cup. I drink like a thirsty shipwreck survivor.

The men look around and have a good laugh when they

see my pee in the pot. In this moment of levity, one slips up and calls the other by his name.

Timofey. It's a clue. I need to make friends with him, make him identify with me, appear helpless, and prey on his emotions. Maybe, just maybe, I can weasel my way out of this hole.

~

"Where is the man who visit you?" Timofey asks in broken English. His face is close to mine. The smell of sardines and vodka on his breath.

My instinct is to turn away, but instead, I give him a blank stare.

"Don't make me hurt you. You're very pretty. Ballerina, no?" he grabs my chin. I pull away and kick him in the leg.

He growls and knocks me in the jaw, sending me backward causing my head to slam against the brick wall. My cheek burns, and my head throbs.

His partner speaks harshly to him. I don't understand all the words, but I get the impression the other guy doesn't want my face marred. These two must be henchmen, and the person in charge probably has an interest in preserving my looks.

"Don't play stupid. I know your friend. He has many names. You know him as Riccardo."

Now it's starting to make sense. Riccardo is who they want. This confirms my suspicion Riccardo is involved in something shady. These guys are just using me to get to him. They're looking for intel and probably using me as bait. If Riccardo doesn't take the bait, they will either let me go or kill me.

"Answer me," he screams in my face and slaps me again.

My ears are ringing, and I bite my tongue to prevent myself from crying. I won't give these men the satisfaction

"I don't know anything," I scream back at him.

"Ah, we know he visits you. You and he have good fuck?" He nudges his accomplice, sharing a chuckle at my expense.

"Yes, he visited me. I don't know why he's here or where he is." That's the truth. but I doubt they believe me.

"Why? What does he want?"

"I have no idea."

"You think on it. We'll be back." Timofey grunts and tosses a brown paper bag into my lap.

They leave. I shiver. Dammit, I should've asked for a blanket. I'm cold, and my face is throbbing. It's a good thing I don't have a mirror to see how bad it looks. My cheek is on fire, so I press it against the cold cellar wall hoping it will help with the swelling.

Later, when my stomach starts to complain, I opened the bag to find a turkey and Swiss cheese sandwich on rye with a side of coleslaw. I hate cabbage, and I hate rye but I force myself to eat both. There's no telling how long I'm going to be here, and I need to eat to keep up my strength.

Dammit. I never had a chance to phone the director of the ballet troupe. As far as I know, no one is looking for me.

15

RICCARDO

"It's late, she's not picking up," I want to scream in frustration but I'm staring at Dante as I pace over the expensive rugs. For all I know, she's being rebellious and sitting at home ignoring my calls and texts. I chastise myself for thinking she's self-absorbed in that way. She's immersed in her career as a dancer. Hell, she's never screwed anyone.

Across the room, Sal and Francesca bring Massimo up to speed while the rest of our men are outside, hiding the weapons in underground bunkers made to store food from the farm in the cool months, along with homemade canned goods and possibly cured meat.

"Riccardo, can you think of anyone here who would want to harm her?" he asks because neither of us can rule out an abduction.

"Of course not, but this has Ignazio's fingerprints all over it," I reply. My heart is racing with the same fear I felt so many years ago in Israel.

"Francesca, let's take a ride. We need to go to Liat's apartment and see if she's there." Dante taps her elbow for her to follow us. He grabs his coat and swings it on in a seamless move only he can manage. I'm close behind and help Francesca into her coat before grabbing my own.

"Let me grab a gun." Francesca ducks into the hallway and returns, stuffing the gun into the back of her jeans. I must admit she looks good in a dark wig.

Dante chuckles. "You need a t-shirt with that printed on it."

"Right?" she quips and hollers to Sal announcing she'll be back.

Sal gives his fiancée a quizzical look before returning to his debate with Massimo about what they should eat for dinner. I close the door as they head into the kitchen.

I can't eat until I know Liat is safe.

"It's getting late," I comment as I type Liat's address into my GPS and back the car out of the garage.

"So, what's up? You and Dante have been like Siamese twins since I arrived." Francesca asks as she looks around. Even though it's dark and desolate outside, she's paying attention to everything. This is her first time in Russia, and she's soaking it up like a sponge.

"My ward might be missing.

"How long?"

"She had a ballet performance earlier today. Can you look it up online and see if she was still the headliner?"

"I don't have any bars," she replies holding her phone up, in hopes of a better signal.

"We need to get to this Krill Volkov. He's the son of the Bratva King who runs this city. Word has it he may be able to help us get rid of Ignazio."

"Great. Where is he?" she asks, eager to help.

"We'll find him. His father is Vladislav Volkov and Ignazio's latest lover."

"Great, let's hope Vladislav is someone who likes to show off his ill-gotten gains. I'll have Sal find his money and transfer it to Ignazio's account. One thing oligarchs don't like is losing money," she adds matter-of-factly.

That's why I like her so much, she's always direct.

"Sounds like a good plan. Simple–clear cut," Dante interjects as he checks his gun to make sure it's loaded.

"I'll be the one to go in, it won't be as obvious as you, Riccardo. I assume you've already been to her place on this trip?"

Francesca's right, but it's annoying I'm so predictable, or is it that she's so fucking perceptive?

"Yes, foolishly, I went there to tell her it wasn't safe here, and she needed to go home."

"Not to make you feel any worse, but showing up at her flat didn't help matters."

I can tell she's not happy I blew my cover and jeopardized the whole operation. A rookie mistake, and I'm too fucking old to be a rookie or make mistakes that are as obvious as the nose of my face.

"Ignazio doesn't know anything, so we're fine."

"Are we? If Ignazio knows about Liat, then she's on the lookout for us. There is no end to what that woman can do and who she can reach."

Ignazio hates Dante for bringing her daughter Juliet into his mafia world. We didn't even know she existed until their engagement. Since then, she has been a constant thorn in our side and a worthy adversary.

"Which is why we're all here," Dante reminds us to keep ourselves calm and focused on our mission. Unfortunately, the past can't be undone with a turnkey like Harry Potter.

"No offense, Riccardo," Francesca pats my shoulder to make amends for pointing out my actions may have triggered a snare. Liat is probably paying the price for it as we stand around helpless.

I respect Francesca's demeanor and love the fact that she's even more dangerous when she's pissed. I want her pissed as hell if it means I'll see Liat again, and end Ignazio's life once and for all.

"We're almost there," I announce as I circle the block. Without a word, we're all on the lookout for suspicious cars parked where they shouldn't be. I don't trust this place or the people. I wish we had drawn Ignazio to us in Italy and met on our own turf.

Francesca murmurs, "Let me out, what is her flat number?"

"Fifty-two oh' one. Fifth floor."

"Great, if I'm not back in ten minutes, we've got a party."

Outside the building, she pulls her hoodie over her head, wraps her coat tighter to her toned body to stay warm, and waits outside the building for someone to let her in.

"This waiting is killing me," I grumble. Sitting here gives me too much time to think the worst. I drive off, go down one block, and continue making right turns until we're back to where we started.

"Riccardo, we've all had these moments. Remember, just because this feels familiar doesn't mean it will have the same outcome."

"It's not like. . ." I protest without having the words to continue.

"Just hang in there. I don't see anyone waiting for us here. That's a good sign."

Dante and I have been through years of sketchy operations. Like when Juliet's father was after her, and Dante protected her against the odds. That took a few years off my life. As his right-hand adviser and confidant, I'm the one who takes care of him, not the other way around.

"Francesca is coming out," Dante's enthusiasm is short-lived when we see Liat isn't with her.

As soon as she gets in the car, I ask, "Well?"

"Her bag was packed. I found it under the bed. I couldn't find a passport, ID, or cellphone."

Francesca's words feel like a punch to the gut. Fear and guilt are so crushing it's hard to breathe. I grind my teeth.

"I'll see if we can hack into the building CCTV, but I doubt it. What was the plan, Riccardo?"

"She's off tomorrow, she was to fly out tonight, after the show. Then she was going to call the ballet director from Italy to say she had a family emergency."

"If she's off tomorrow, her co-workers won't notice she's gone for forty-eight hours. That's convenient." Francesca pauses. "Who could be using Liat to get to you?"

"I have no clue. Maybe it's Ignazio. She's like a goddamn plague, everywhere and yet, nowhere at the same time. And she has nine fucking lives."

"Yeah. I agree," Dante seconds my sentiment, having known her firsthand.

"What is in your past? Something has to link you to Ignazio. Have you had any run-ins with Russians in the past?" Francesca pushes me.

"I don't know," I slam my fist into the steering wheel in frustration before heading back to our safe house. I'm beginning to wonder if anything is safe at this juncture.

"There was an arms dealer from Russia who may have been involved in the incident that killed my wife and friends. We never found out who the main guy was behind the bombing. All we ever heard was a name. Phantom."

"Are you fucking kidding me? What is this? A DC comic strip character? It's not funny, but seriously? What the fuck is a real-life Phantom?"

"I don't have a clue."

"The clock is ticking. We will split up the team, so someone can meet with Krill. When we make contact, Ignazio will be under surveillance, or, better yet, let's see if we can get access to her house cameras and schedule. We need to get in and out quickly."

"And we have to find Liat."

"We have to move fast, be methodical, and yet, not spook anyone," Francesca adds.

"I met one of her friends from the theatre. His name is Aleksandr. She liked him, but he seemed a little off if you ask me."

"Oh, Riccardo, you actually met people in her life?"

"It was innocent. I saw her perform. He was there. Ignazio was there too with the Governor, Volkov, in the balcony."

"Fuck." Dante's Italian temper explodes.

"Don't worry. She didn't see me."

"No, of course not. But you put us all at risk by showing your face when you have no clue who is involved. These unscrupulous people infiltrate every level of society and will not hesitate to turn in their own mother or brother."

"What the fuck, Riccardo? When were you going to tell us?"

"I've been consumed with Liat. I didn't think it was important other than to say I have visual confirmation Ignazio and her lover are here."

"Are they holding Liat for ransom or to bait you?" Francesca ponders.

"Where do we go from here?" I ask because it's the first

time I don't have a move. The stakes are so high, I'm para-
lyzed with indecision.

16

———

LIAT

The chill in my bones wakes me. Everything hurts from being in one position, and as much as I don't want to move, I must. It will help to keep me warm. I struggle to my feet and pace back and forth like a caged tiger.

This solitary confinement with no end in sight is maddening. Now I understand why people in captivity scratch marks on a wall to keep track of the days. I have nothing to distinguish one hour from the next, in this room with no windows, let alone one day from another.

What would I give to be in Florence with the warmth of the Tuscan sun on my face? I worry about Aunt Vivian and my cousins in Italy and hope they are safe. I've been so consumed with my own problems, I failed to consider they might be in danger as well.

I try to jiggle the wooden door open; it won't budge. They'd be too foolish for that, not that I anticipated it would open. I jam my shoulder up against it, and I bounce off, the event sends me reeling backward. I push hair out of my face and break down, crying tears of frustration. The door must be padlocked from the other side, and these doors are ancient, meant to withstand a second coming.

Hearing the jingle of metal keys and footsteps approaching, I scurry to my familiar spot against the wall and wipe my eyes on my coat sleeve.

Timofey enters, holding a blanket under his arm. I meet his mean eyes filled with ungodly deeds. He throws the smelly object at me, and I catch it between my handcuffed hands. It's a nappy thing but better than nothing. I'll take this as an indication they want to keep me alive, for now.

Opening his thermos, he pours me a cup of something steamy and hands it to me. I sniff, and it smells like tea. I'm thankful for the warmth but dread the thought of staying awake from the caffeine.

I finish it and hold the empty cup out for more. Timofey refills it.

Between sips, I ask, "What do they want with me?"

"It's not for me to tell you."

"You must know something," suggesting he's not in the loop and trying to provoke him to say more.

"I know you need to behave."

"You can't slap me anymore?"

"Oh, we have other means that don't leave a mark."

"What is it you want to know?" I feign innocence and compliance. It seems to be what they want.

"Give up Riccardo's location and his contacts."

"I don't know anything. I told you. I was never told what he did on his own time. He's here to see me perform, that's it."

"Bullshit." He takes my cup, throws what tea is left on the floor, and turns to leave.

"Thank you for the blanket. It's cold in here."

"It's supposed to be cold in here." He opens the door and disappears, and my dreams of an escape go with him.

I pray to a God I don't believe in, begging to be let out. I was raised Catholic but haven't been to church in years. I love going to Cathedrals because I appreciate their beauty and architecture, but I no longer go there to worship.

I murmur another prayer this will all have been a bad dream when I wake up.

I must've dozed off because the sound of keys rouses me. When the door opens, I pretend to be asleep.

"Wake up. I need information."

I feel a boot nudge my shoulder and open my eyes to see Timofey's partner. He's holding a dirty pillowcase filled with something. With the tattoo of a snake on his neck, he doesn't exactly look like Santa Claus.

"I don't know anything. Just let me go."

"I don't think so. Tell me what I want. Where is Riccardo?"

"I can't give you what you want." I sit up and meet his eyes in a never-ending stare.

"Right." He dumps the contents of the pillowcase, and hardback books tumble onto the floor. He picks up two of them, puts them together, and smacks me upside the head.

I cry out and cower on the floor against the wall. He continues to hit my back and shoulders with the books so many times I lose count. Until, with a burst of energy, I grab at his ankle and pull. Catching him off guard, he falls on his butt. In his anger, he kicks me and throws the two books at my head.

"Take that, you bitch. It won't get any easier for you," he rages before slamming the door behind him and locking it.

I collect my blanket and use a portion of it as a makeshift pillow, and the rest I pull over me. I can't sit anymore, deciding to curl into a fetal position on the cement floor bed. Feeling completely demoralized and less than human, I murmur prayers to myself to not go insane with worrying over my fate.

17

RICCARDO

We enter the safe house, and Massimo greets us holding a glass of whiskey. "How bad is the situation?"

To question how he knows it's bad, is immaterial. We have a sixth sense with each other. He's no novice at this, and his grandfather is a revered man in the Albanian mafia with the largest reach internationally.

"It's bleak. We can't find Liat. We checked her apartment, and it looks like she has been taken. She has a friend, Aleksandr. I want to find him and see what he knows. That might get us some clues." I rake my fingers through my hair and realize I haven't stopped in more than twelve hours. My eyes feel like sandpaper.

"You're wiped, Riccardo. Take a shower, get some rest," Sal suggests.

"I can't eat. I can't sleep. Time is ticking away," I reply, out of exhaustion.

"We'll get an address on this guy, Aleksandr. You, shower," Massimo commands before he takes a swig of his whiskey.

I nod and walk towards the room where I left my stuff. A hot shower will clear my head. I shuck my clothes and don't care where they land. I turn on the shower, and when it's warm enough, I let the water work its magic.

After I've dried, I take my time shaving over the round glass bowl sink. I hate myself more with each swipe of the razor and chastise myself for not keeping away from Liat.

My years of experience tell me Ignazio has Liat. No one else has a reason to take her, and Ignazio has resources we don't if she's that high up in the Russian hierarchy. Was this her reason for hooking up with someone so powerful here?

Feeling a little better, I look for everyone and find them hovering over the dining room table, strategizing. They have figured out where Aleksandr lives. He's not an accomplished player by any means. He didn't impress me as one capable of betrayal, either.

Enzo and Massimo take off in the car to round him up. I can't be seen, so I stay here at the farm, where the situation eats away at me. I'm helpless to do anything until they get back.

Dante pours a scotch. I swipe it off the table and pace the room. I can't sit, who could sit at a time like this? I look over Sal's shoulder at the map they've drawn. It's scrawled across the front page of the "Pravda's" propaganda-filled newspaper. From what I can see, Aleksandr lived only a few blocks from Liat. That little prick better know where she is.

It's late, I walk outside. I want a cigarette, but there is no reason to relapse when I've worked so hard for it. It would only be a temporary fix. My eyes burn, I've been up for so long. But until Liat is safe, I won't be able to rest. I button my coat and stare at the white moon with clouds passing over it and wonder if she can see it too.

Dante says, "I got a call; they found the kid. Turns out,

his father has a huge gambling problem and got in debt with the Volkov's. He made a deal to save his own skin. They were after you all along. No wonder we were easy to set up, Ignazio knows everything about us. The Russians have access to everything through international associations like NATO and Interpol. She can circumvent the system. I'll make a call to Marchello to make sure they keep their guard up in Italy."

"It's two in the morning."

"Good, he'll be home." He pats my back as encouragement.

As I absorb this new information, fear takes hold because Liat is in a precarious position. I'm not sure we can get to her, but I'll find her even if it kills me.

Kicking at the rocks in the dirt feels good to release some anger. I kick another and another like a kid skipping stones. Only it's not as simple but going through the motion seems to calm my nerves for the moment.

"Riccardo, come in, it's cold," Francesca hollers.

Now that she mentions it, she's right. I'm not dressed for this weather and turn my feet towards the house.

"Lay down, even if you can't sleep, your body needs a break. I have a sleeping pill. Take it. The rest of us will carry on. You can't do this alone. We'll work around the clock, I promise." She hands me a tiny pill and bottled water.

She's right. There's no use refusing. I won't be good to anyone if my mind's not clear. I'll only be out for a few hours.

I AWAKE to the familiar smells of breakfast being cooked. Worried I may have slept too long, I leap out of bed and throw on jeans and a DriFit shirt to combat the cold. I slip on socks and tactical boots before joining the others at the table.

"Fill me in," I plead urgently.

"We know where Aleksandr dropped Liat off. We aren't sure where to go from there, but Sal has a few addresses in the neighborhood. I wouldn't be surprised if Ignazio isn't waiting for us with a surprise of her own," Dante cuts into over-easy eggs and crunches on bacon.

"We'll do surveillance today," Sal adds. "A prisoner has to be taken care of and, we know it must be the Bratva. Could be police or hired goons," he shrugs.

"It has to be the Bratva. Ignazio's fucking the head guy," Francesca scoffs as she squeezes fresh orange juice. I'd hate to be her orange as her skilled assassin hands render the fruit lifeless.

"We'll find her, Riccardo," Dante reassures me.

"We need to see if Nikolay can help us."

"It's dangerous, what if his allegiance is to Ignazio, or she's untouchable by order of his father?" Massimo asks with concern.

"Good point. We have nothing to lose. She will know I didn't come alone."

Everyone looks at me like I'm a traitor. "What?"

Dante pushes his empty plate away and says, "We think this might be about you. Years ago, our lives intersected by chance, but maybe we were linked by Ignazio all along. You admit you don't know the Russians involved in your Middle East gun deal."

"No. Ignazio would have been young."

"Young and angry," Francesca huffs. "She gave up her daughter because my father was a psycho, and she'd never be free or safe, nor would Juliet. Ignazio is intelligent, and her linguistic skills enable her to live anywhere and infiltrate any government or criminal organization virtually undetected since she can create a new identity with a perfect background check. It's ingenious."

"That's not what I want to hear." Knowing I need something in the tank, I take a few bites of bacon. "I'll let you handle surveillance, but we have to find Liat today. I don't care if we have to toss the city," my voice, angry and impatient, doesn't go without notice.

Francesca is the first to speak, "I'll work with Dante on the meeting with Nikolay. We heard from John last night. He loves money, and we have a ton of it. We have confirmation of the opulent residence the Governor lives in as well."

I nod. Looks like the team was working all night.

"Francesca and Sal will carry out surveillance. I'll go with Massimo to meet Nikolay. We know where he goes to the gym and pool daily. We can inquire about signing up. Drop a few lines and see if he bites," Dante suggests with his usual confidence.

"Great. I'm here with my dick in my hand," I scoff.

"Better to have it in your hand, than have Ignazio cut it off," Massimo jokes. "In case you haven't noticed, I think she wants you dead."

"Fuck," I mutter.

18

RICCARDO

Dante and Massimo leave with a man from the Belarus mafia who will drive them to the place where they hope to make contact with Nikolay. I pray Nikolay isn't insane, and maybe he'll take favor with us. Why? I have no clue. If he's smart, he might be on to Ignazio.

In my heart of hearts, I know she has a million camouflages, and she can shed them like a snake sheds its skin. But eventually, she'll want recognition for her brilliance and cunningness.

She's a cunt, and I can't wait to put a bullet between her eyes. No matter her reason, no matter what her tie is to the past, I won't rest until she's gone. She has to die.

Francesca, Sal, and I set out to watch the neighborhood where Liat is assumed to be. The sun is coming over the horizon. I long to see her and chastise her for being cold and indifferent after I took her virginity. No matter the situation, she was on Ignazio's radar. For how long, I can't be sure. I may never know. In the end, it doesn't matter.

I let Francesca drive the van we borrowed. It has a shipping company's logo on the side of it. In the back are other members of our crew. Enzo is Massimo's guard. He's sitting in the midst of technology in which I have no clue about. All those gadgets and wires give me a headache. Normally, I hire those services out, but now Francesca is on our team, and Sal has developed a penchant for hacking more than bank accounts. The team we have put together is like having six extra people with indispensable skill sets.

Before long we're driving through a suburb of modest houses. Sal and Francesca pull out binoculars and wear a communication device in one ear like the secret service. Everyone communicates in Italian in case the Russians are listening they won't understand what we're saying. Brilliant.

Francesca has a can of spray paint in her hand as she and Sal exit the van. I'm told not to move until the cameras are blacked out.

Enzo is monitoring their conversation and rattles off quickly. "They think they found where she is."

"I have to be there."

"Sure, sure," he replies into the radio before taking off his headset and following me out of the van.

I pull my gun out to make sure it's loaded, jam it in a holster on my waist, and cover it with my coat. I force myself to walk and not run so as not to elicit attention from anyone in the houses I pass. I have plenty of rubles in my pocket to pay them off if it comes to that. Silence is golden.

Enzo shows me where the house is and points out the cellar where Francesca is picking the lock. The door swings open and we see a figure cowering in a corner.

I rush past my friends and get there first. She's shielding her face. I have to make sure it's her. I cup her head and turn her towards me.

She shakes but moves her hands from her eyes. Her eyes

are tired. Her face is swollen and red. I take her hand, it's cold.

"Liat. I've got you. It's me. Are you okay?"

"I knew you'd find me. I just didn't know how long it would take. Be careful. There are two men who come and go."

"Shush. Save your strength." I scoop her into my arms, she's fragile and her eyes are wide with shock.

"Thank God," Francesca comments as she looks about the room. I know it's a killing room as I smell the dried blood, sweat, and urine from years of unspeakable atrocities. The criminals are brazened to carry out acts of torture in these houses, in daylight no less.

We situate ourselves in the van, and Francesca brings over a medical kit. Why didn't I think of that?

"You're going to be fine," I repeat over and over.

Liat begins to cry, she sniffles and tries to speak but chokes on her words. "I," she swallows, "They hit me, beat me with books. I hurt all over."

Francesca hands me a cloth, wet with antiseptic as the van moves through the traffic.

"You're safe. You'll never leave my side again." I blot her scrapes and check for broken bones. She's weak but she's in one piece and still has full use of her extremities. For that, I'm thankful.

Francesca hands me warm tea and Liat tries to sit up but is unable. I hold her up and feed it to her. "Take small sips. Easy does it."

She falls against my chest and closes her eyes. Francesca gives her some muscle relaxers to swallow. "Take it. You'll feel better."

Sal is driving, "How safe is our safe house now?"

"I think we're okay. I think Ignazio couldn't find me, so

she took Liat. Does anyone have news from Dante or Massimo?

"Negative," Enzo replies taking off his headphones. "They can't meet wired. We wait."

I nod and smooth my hand over Liat's long hair not caring that it hasn't been washed in days. She brings out the best in me and I pull her to me because I can't resist. I hug her as if my life depends on it. Maybe it does. She's my reason for living.

When we finally get to the house, I put Liat in my bed. Taking off her coat and her clothes, I'm sickened by the blue and purple bruises on her legs, arms, and back. She tries to speak.

"Rest. I'll put you in a shirt and keep you warm. You need rest."

She mumbles and is out. I cover her with all the blankets on the bed and only when I'm satisfied she's in a deep sleep, do I leave.

Seeing Sal and Francesca I say, "Thank you so much. You two are incredible."

"Thanks, but we're family. Are you going to tell us what she really is to you?" Sal fishes for answers.

"Nope." I smile now that the threat against her life has ended. I go to the door, pull out a wad of rubles and hand it to the Belarusian guard. I instruct him to defend the house and make sure the young woman stays inside. He nods in agreement.

"Alright, back to work, where are we on Ignazio's daily routine?"

"Not too much," Enzo replies. "She likes to swim and shop. No surprise there. And she has a guard with her at all times or her boyfriend."

"I don't know how we take her out without starting a war with the Bratva."

"Well, she's not Bratva. She's not married to him. I suggest you set up new accounts with her name on them."

"I'm on it," Sal replies eagerly to help and grabs his encrypted laptop.

Francesca hands me warm tea and I sip. My lips are dry. My nerves are raw and I'm jittery. I can't tell if it's the elation of finding Liat, holding her again, or the fact that I might have a second chance with her. Even if she doesn't want me, she's alive and we'll work past the trauma.

"You love her," she speaks softly, conveying more emotion than I thought possible from an assassin.

"Possibly. I'm too old for her. What do I know?"

"I know love when I see it. One has to experience it to see it. I never had real love until Sal."

"Mm," I grunt. My old self will have a difficult time giving up my solitude and living a life outside of the family business. "I'm not sure I can measure up to Liat's romantic version of a couple."

"It will come, give it time."

19

RICCARDO

Liat sits up in bed as I knock and open the door carrying a tray of food and hot tea.

"You need to eat. How do you feel?"

"Like a truck ran over me. Every muscle in my body hurts. How did you find me?"

"Don't worry about it. You are not to step outside, I will make sure you are not taken again. I have a guard at the door, so if you defy me, he will notify me, and you will be escorted back into the house," I speak sternly.

"Fine."

Hm. No argument. I kind of miss her giving me shit.

"But I'll come and go as I please, with a bodyguard, when I'm better."

That's my girl. "Agreed. It will be me most of the time. I'm not letting you out of my sight. After you eat, the shower is in there, and Francesca gave you some of her clothes. She thinks the spandex will fit. You're too thin."

"I'm fine. Has anyone from the ballet noticed I'm gone?" Her eyes implore me. I'm sure she's worried about her career.

"Aleksandr gave them some excuse. Francesca found your luggage, your passport, and ID are gone. We'll have to fix that so we can get home."

"Shit. Why did he do this?"

"Aleksandr supported his mother and brother while his father gambled and drank everything away. He was in debt with the Bratva, and this was a way to repay them before they hurt him or his father."

A tear slips from her eye. She wipes it away, putting on a brave face despite the betrayal.

"Did you love him?" My question is to the point. I hold my breath waiting for her answer.

"No, he liked me. He wanted to go to New York. Maybe they promised that as part of his deal. I've never been so close to someone, we clicked. We were best friends, but I was never attracted to him like that," her eyes remain on the food she moves around the plate. Her eyes have dark rings under them, but they're beautiful as she lifts them to meet mine. When I meet her eyes, I still see the fear from her ordeal. She lifts a shoulder as if she's shy before turning her gaze to focus on the tea.

I know her so well, and yet, not at all. Are my feelings new, or were they there all along? I've always considered her off-limits. It's taboo to have my heart skip a beat when she walks in the room, knowing I shouldn't touch her but wanting to protect her at all costs. I also want to ravage her body with kisses and caresses. Her smile lights my world. I have a great poker face. Even so, Dante wasn't surprised that I gave in to temptation. He also noticed Liat's adoration for me years ago.

How will I know she's sure I'm the one for her? How long can it last? I shake my head as if it's stiff before I rub my neck.

"Are you okay?" I can't mistake the concern in her voice, I'm supposed to be taking care of her and I can't let my guard down now. She needs me to find these men and kill them.

"Yes, it was a rough night. We're lucky the place they were holding you was so obvious. I thought for sure it was a trap. Do you remember anything about the two men who abducted you?"

"Yes," she moves the tray off her lap. "One was called Timofey. They were both Russian. Timofey hit my jaw, and the other one beat me with books. They kept asking where you were and what you were doing in Russia. Why are they looking for you?" She's finished her tea and is nibbling on eggs.

"Um. Well." I decide after everything she's been through deserves an honest answer.

"I'm here to track down a woman who has a vendetta with the Micheli family, and she's made it clear she has a beef with me, too." I rub my hand over my goatee. "I don't know why."

"I don't understand how I became involved in this. Is she Russian?" her innocent eyes implore me.

"No, worse, Sicilian," I chuckle. "She will stop at nothing and use you to get to me, I assume."

"You're involved with the mafia."

I search her face. What does she know?

"How do you know?"

"I can do a search online. I overheard you and your sister talking in hushed tones over the years. That's when a kid really listens. I wanted to know why you were gone all the time."

"Sorry about that. It was to keep you safe."

"Or was it to keep you safe, too?" her voice is stronger.

She puts down her fork and sets the tray aside. Outside of the purple and yellow bruises, I'd never know what she's been subjected to. More importantly, she's engaging in our conversations, not sinking in despair or depression. These are encouraging signs that she'll rebound without a long recovery. Her bruised face pains me. If I find this Timofey, he's a dead man.

"Yeah, well. I'll take this tray out of here." I pull the tray into my hands. "Shower, take your time."

Fuck. The thought of her in the shower turns me on.

I pass through to the kitchen, and the main door opens. Massimo and Dante are talking between themselves before they call out to us.

"Well? How did it go?" Francesca is the first to question the new arrivals.

"Good, we think," Dante smiles at me. "I heard you all found Liat?"

"Yes," I exhale in relief that we're all under one roof.

"Great, I can't wait to meet her," he replies just as Liat enters the room.

"Wow, who is everyone?" Her eyes surmise my boss. "You must be Dante," she extends her hand. "Liat."

"Dante," he shakes her hand. "How are you feeling? I'm so relieved and happy you are fine."

"Thank you."

"This is Massimo, my half-brother, and over there, the one who looks like us is my brother Sal."

Francesca mutters something about hens that need baking, and the women disappear into the kitchen.

It's afternoon, and the sun is already going down. It's weird being this far north. I'm over all this cold weather and gray skies.

"What do we know? Is Krill going to help us?" I ask

impatiently, anxious to be done with this mess and get the hell out of this country.

"Who says we saw him?" Massimo says to be a pain in my ass.

"If you return without completing the mission, I will kick your ass out until it's done," I reply in no mood to play around.

"True," Dante acknowledges my ruthlessness, "And you are in luck," he says smugly. "We met him at his coffee house. His thoughts are run more Westernized than I expected. He has expensive taste judging from his watch and nice Audie. He doesn't dress like our Belarusian friends in black tracksuits. No flashy gold around his neck. He's smart and speaks as if he's educated. He made it clear he wanted Ignazio out of his father's life. He has siblings he doesn't trust around her. Not to mention he doesn't trust her around anyone he cares about. Did I say he doesn't trust her?" he quips to be funny, making it more amusing as he's typically more stoic and has a dry sense of humor. "Smart man," he reiterates as he pours whiskey from a crystal decanter that must have cost thousands of rubles.

"I'm sure Krill is going to check us out. With so many of his father's men in Ignazio's pocket, he'll determine he's better off with us," Massimo states confidently.

I like his jovial mood. Only his wife can get him to horse around and laugh in mirth, and she's not here. If he's confident Krill will be an asset, it's a good sign. It's a break we need, and if it pans out, our job won't be as daunting.

"What's next?" I run a hand over the map on the dining room table we're hovering over.

"We'll see what the surveillance cameras at the house picked up. Krill believes that Ignazio makes his father look weak. There is no forgiveness in the Bratva. She's been trying to tell him how to run his business. And a point of interest, they have been arguing." Massimo taps a pen on the table as we all glance at the layout Francesca penned of the Volkov compound.

"Massimo, Sal, Francesca. Can you provide reconnaissance on the house?"

"Sure," Massimo answers before the others get a word on the matter.

"Great." I'm on my game again, my mind is flying. "Sal, let's set up those fake bank accounts and siphon off the same amount from each of Vladislav's accounts. Dante, tell Krill that he needs to say something to his father that compels him to look at his money."

"Sure thing. We have burner phones; I expect to hear from him this afternoon. We need to find out where Ignazio is most vulnerable."

"And what concessions have we made to Krill?" Francesca asks as she drinks bottled water. None of us trust the water from an unsecured source.

"Tons of coke, some weapons, and the promise that we won't harm his father."

"Fair enough. I assume everyone has work to do before dinner." I stand to indicate we're done. This should clear out the house leaving Liat and me alone for a few hours.

My cock twitches in anticipation. I'm as excited as a teenager with the experience of an accomplished lover. Will Liat still want me?

20

RICCARDO

When I enter our room, Liat sits on the bed, her knees pulled to her chin, arms wrapped tightly around them. She used to do this as a child when she needed consoling.

I casually approach, deciding to treat her as a person who didn't go through a horrendous ordeal. Cautiously, I sit at her feet.

"What can I do to make you feel better?"

"Hold me, Riccardo," her voice, uneven.

Silently, I move closer, pull her into my arms, and kiss the top of her head.

"Did you tell me everything?" I pray that they didn't rape her. Surely, she would admit it if it did happen. Or would she? She's one to put on a brave face to protect me.

"Yes," her arms slide around my fitted thermal shirt that clings to my mature torso. She tilts her head back, leaving her lips parted.

"Liat. . ." I can't finish. A rush of emotions hit me at once. It's a tidal wave as the dam breaks, I'm at a loss for words.

My lips are on hers before I can think. There is nothing

in my head but thoughts of her, hormones going crazy as my cock fills my jeans.

"I have to have you, Liat." I lean her back on the bed.

"I know." She kisses my neck, her hands snake around my neck as I loom over her.

I peel off her shirt and bra, her breasts are beautiful. I take a nipple in my mouth as my tongue plays with it, enjoying it, giving it a nip before I move on to her earlobe. My thumb rubs over her nipple, back and forth, until her nipple is firm. A flick of my thumb over her nipple one last time as she moans.

I push my hand between her legs. I feel her lips through the pliable material. My fingers move over the seam covering her clit. Forcing my fingers to add more pressure, I rub her until her wetness seeps through the material.

Satisfied with the results, I pull my fingers to my lips, licking them as I stare into her soft eyes. I'm in love with this modern woman. I have no right to be rewarded with her, but it won't stop me from taking her whenever I want, as often as I want.

I tug her leggings and socks off and run my hand slowly up her leg as if it's a forbidden fruit; I rake my nails into her skin lightly, to leave the lingering flesh wanting more. I've reached the desired effect when I see her back rising off the duvet. She makes to draw her legs together and move them to one side as she withers under me, but I clap my hand on one knee, forcing it apart so I can suckle her.

I lick her, enjoying her sweetness as I clamp a hand under her buttocks, digging into it with my nails in my desire to take her quickly, but I fight it off. Hard thrusts are better at times, but not now.

Liat pulls my head to her, no doubt it's a move to calm her state of pre-orgasm. I don't object to getting her off with my talented tongue, but I want her to grip my cock with her tight pussy and spill my seed in her when I climax.

She slips her hand down my shirt, then unleashes my belt, loosens my jeans, unzips me, and slides her hand into my boxers, where she grabs my cock.

He feels the attention and his cock fills with more blood, making him larger than I thought possible. The pleasure is a preamble to the release he desires, pre-come wets his head.

I pull away to kneel. "Take me," I command.

Liat lurches into action, giving him a hard stroke before going down on my swollen, and needy, cock. The bed dips as I lean back letting out a deep moan. Her lips tighten around me as her head bobs. She caresses my bulging head, with circular flicks with her tongue, more skilled than a virgin. No doubt, she's learned through friends or research.

She takes me to the brink of coming before breaking away abruptly.

"I have to have you, now," my voice reflects my urgency due to my shallow breaths of anticipation.

I flip her onto her stomach, push my jeans down, and thrust my cock into her. She's warm and inviting, a second home for my hard cock. My mind floats, I force myself to move slowly, controlling myself as I glide in and out of her.

I place my palm in the middle of her back before thrusting deeper. She lets out a whimper, then a moan of pleasure as I hold her motionless under me.

She gasps for air between my thrusts and twists her buttocks, putting my cock in a new position that is even more pleasurable than the last. Her inner goddess holds my cock captive, her muscles pulsate around me, and I know she's about to come.

"Come when I tell you." I quicken my pace, forcing her to contain the rising tide that's building inside her pussy.

Her pussy quivers around me, smaller ones leading to larger ones, I place two fingers on her nub and apply pressure. "Now."

She screams as her orgasm crests like a wave from a typhoon, her wetness drenches my cock and drips over my fingers. I continue to rub her until I release myself with a long moan, my body convulsing at its intensity.

I recover, catching my breath as she's spent, panting under me.

"Fuck," she murmurs.

"You can say that again," I smile as I roll her onto her back and take her lips on mine. "Did you like it?"

"Mind-blowing," she chuckles.

21

RICCARDO

We gather around the table like it's Sunday dinner in Italy, only we're freezing our balls off here. Dante hangs up with Juliet while Francesca and Liat carry food to the table.

I find a bottle of wine and fill a glass for everyone. John, our host, earned his rubles and euros for stocking the house. I facilitated a list for him so we wouldn't have to eat cabbage and meat pies the entire visit. We're out of the city, but we're not living in a tent, so I made sure we'd be comfortable.

"Ignazio must have dumped her original man when she learned she could move up to bigger fish. The Governor of St. Petersburg is a huge catch and gives her unfettered access to more than I could ever hope to obtain. The Russians have an unprecedented reach and resources," Sal ponders with his thoughts as we dig into the meat and potatoes.

The girls made a mixed green salad, and I'll be damned if I can identify a single item except for tomatoes.

I walk around the table, refilling wine glasses that are empty already. "It makes sense. She's one to hustle. There is no telling how many bodies she's left dead in Europe." I realize this is the wrong thing to bring up so soon after Liat's ordeal. I quickly shift my eyes to her as wine trickles down the outside of the glass I'm filling. "I'm sorry, Liat."

She shrugs, "I had little hope I'd come out alive. I want her dead just like you," her voice is strong, determined. Our eyes meet, both of us resilient, and we don't need words to explain it. My cock twitches. I love her spunk and can't wait to get this mess behind us, so I can fuck her all over Italy.

"Glad to hear it," Dante raises his wine glass. "To a successful mission."

We chime in with 'salute' and sip before we continue to discuss business.

I finished my job as the beverage director settling into my chair next to hers. I squeeze her hand under the table, giving her encouragement. I thumb the inside of her palm until she grabs my hand. I imagine she's wet remembering how I went down on her, and she can't bear it anymore.

I slip her a knowing smile. She blushes as she puts the hand on her lap and proceeds to eat. I'm relieved she's gaining her strength.

"We had a productive day. I normally don't trust others, however, Krill has more to lose than us if Ignazio embezzles money from his father. We both want her out of the picture. When that happens, his father will be able to run his business without interference, something Krill wants for his family. He hates the woman, and he doesn't even know her true past." Dante spits the words out due to his utter disdain for the woman.

"Ignazio excels at pissing people off," Massimo reaffirms the family's disgust for the woman, and the events, that led us here. At least he forgets that Ignazio killed his wife's father just to frame Dante.

"For all we know, she might have Krill on her list along with us," Massimo adds before he throws back more wine. I admire him for being in pristine physical shape. He has to be quick on his feet and strong to overtake opponents larger than him in size.

"How is the data mining going, Sal?" I glance down at the table as he sits next to Francesca. It doesn't escape me that she took her engagement ring off to blend in here. She would be a memorable woman on the streets, even with her wig. Here, only the up-and-coming wealthy people wear the items they purchase with their ill-gotten gains. Smart men of power and wealth fly under the radar like John. No doubt his assets are hidden in various currencies and properties.

Dante looks to his brother Sal, "Can you take Massimo and Francesca to sit on Volkov's house tomorrow? We need to find opportunities for a hit. It has to be where she's vulnerable as we can't risk Valad."

"What if there is only one opportunity?" Liat questions, causing everyone to turn their head to her.

"We can't take it. We don't need Krill and his large family to come for revenge. We'll be in the same place we are now, but instead of one person, there will be many. His cause would be justified, just like us, he'll look for retribution."

I want to run my fingers through her long silky hair, she's taken an interest in my business, and I can't imagine how she understands my life completely. I assume her brush with death has her committed to our eye for an eye mantra.

I'm here for a job, and I can't think past a night of fucking her until she begs me to stop.

"Eat," I murmur.

"I am," she grits her teeth as she replies.

"On a different note, I have seen the word Phantom

come up on the dark web in a Russian chat room. Curious if anyone has heard of it?" Francesca asks. "I was monitoring frequencies to see if Ignazio has the drop on us and this word is not commonplace. I don't know Russian. Maybe one of the men outside can interpret?

My body grows rigid.

"What do you know of it?" I ask in a tone fueled with anger I've suppressed for years.

Her face is one of shock. I'm the calm one in the family. When I'm excited over a situation, it's drastic. She didn't have to be in the family long to understand this. Normally, it's over having a soldier whacked. Drug addiction and stealing are crimes that can't be overlooked.

"Riccardo?" Her voice questions me with concern.

"It's a name I know from an arms deal that yielded great personal loss for me, and I had no idea the person was still around. All this time I thought it had blown. Apparently, I was wrong. Is the chatter picking up?"

"Can't be sure, but it appears so. Is this person a threat to us?"

"We can't dismiss it if that's what you're concerned about. Ignazio showed us an enemy we don't know could do serious harm to us, it's prudent that we proceed with the assumption that we're on the playing field. How many fields there are, is anyone's guess."

"What if it's her? We've discussed the possibility that Ignazio could have been anywhere in the world after my wife was given up for adoption. She was alone, angry, fearful for her life, no doubt." Dante meets Francesca's gaze, "No offense to you, Francesca. Business is business."

"No offense is taken. I hated my father too. The situation made me stronger than him. Thankfully, I didn't inherit his psychotic side."

I let out a chuckle. No, however, she is a damn good assassin.

"What?" Liat questions me.

"Later." She's the only one who doesn't know Francesca is a skilled killer, fighter, and boxer.. and a smart business-woman. I'd love to see the royalty checks she gets off her workout clothing line. She's also the head of the mafia in southern Italy.

"I have too much to live for, we'll go over to the other house, so we don't keep you all awake," Francesca informs everyone of the plans for the evening.

"I have a late-night meeting with Krill, he'll be out with friends at a club tonight, so we can meet innocuously," Dante pushes his plate away. "Riccardo, hold down the fort tonight." His cheeky grin conveys his approval of Liat. Normally, only engaged women would be at our family dinner. It's an odd time for us as a family. Now, Liat is one of us.

"Will do," and agree. I'll step up the guards outside and make it an early night for us. There can only be one woman on my mind when the bedroom door is closed.

"Francesca, I want a full report in the morning. This Phantom is a thorn in my side. I can't rest until I've neutral-ized this person. It could be Ignazio with her penchant for an alias."

"No doubt. I see your concern."

"I'll help with the clean-up," Liat volunteers as she lifts her plate and walks around the table collecting ours.

The men retire to the living room and pretend we're not here. It's fifteen minutes of normalcy. My mind is in a loop over the Phantom. I hope it is Ignazio. It gives me more reasons to kill her.

Everyone disperses.

"Liat, would you like to go on a walk with me? It's cold, but you need fresh air."

She nods, and we dress to brave the chilly evening. We walk around the property under the moon. Enzo follows us with a soldier from our Belarus connection. I feel safer knowing these men know the land. I hope they know who to be on the lookout for and that we're safe. I'm out of our depth here. Everyone looks the same to me, and without help from Giovi, and Massimo's grandfather, who already have connections here, this would have been an impossible feat.

"I'm counting the days until we're back in Italy."

"Me, too." Liat sighs. "It seems like it's been so long. Maybe it's just the bad memories I have of here. It was great up until the point it wasn't."

"Don't dwell on it. I'm the one that carries the past. I don't want that for you. Are you warm enough?" I pull her to me even though she says she's fine. "You need clothing. I'll have Francesca take you shopping tomorrow, I'll be too obvious, and I have work to do. Francesca has disguises, I'd advise you to wear one of her wigs. Do what she tells you to do."

"Yuck," she scoffs.

"Do it for me, it's an order."

"Oh, so I'm to take orders from you now?"

"Absolutely, I can't have my woman showing disrespect."

"That might work in your world, but in mine, a woman is independent."

Independent, my ass. I'll show her who's the boss when we're alone.

"So, am I to follow your every whim?" she taunts me.

"The most important ones, yes."

"And my punishment if I don't?"

"That, my dear, you will have to suffer the consequences."

"We'll see who has the last word," she jests.

"Yes, we will." I'm looking forward to it.

I LOCK THE DOOR, check the cameras, and leave a guard in the kitchen for added insurance. I'm lusting after Liat. I enter the room, she's under the covers, and I can't make out her thoughts. Will she want me? I can't let her go. I haven't let her out of my sight since we rescued her.

"I won't break."

I move to her side, and her hands slide up my shirt. My lips descend on hers as her hand reaches for my hard cock. Her touch is perfect, I shed my trousers so she can grab me. I hold her arms over her head as I lay over her. She fights me, moving her arms, her eyes were wild with rebellion as she glares at me.

I let go of her immediately. I'm a monster for restricting her when thugs tied her up. I can't presume there won't be times that trauma will return.

"It's fine, it's new to me."

"You had a flashback, is what you mean."

"Yes, no. I want to make you happy."

"I pushed you too fast. I'm not good for you."

Her hand caresses my face. "No, you're what I need. I don't want to be treated differently."

She pulls me to her. One kiss is all it takes to bring me back to where we left off. I take my time kissing her lips, outlining her face, and trailing my hand down the side of her shapely body. She probably wants to dance in another city when we get home, but I hate her having to work.

Secretly, I hope that this last tour is enough to fill her quest to be the best. There is more to life than standing in the spotlight.

Liat murmurs under me. I move my hands over her body as if it's the first time I see her naked. Her skin glows as the soft light reflects her beauty. I push my doubts away as my desire takes over. I slide my tongue down her belly as her muscles constrict to resist the urge to buckle under me.

I smile, she's ticklish.

I slip my hand between her thighs, and my tongue caresses her nub. Gently massaging her clit, I lick her. Her back arches, and I slip my hands further under her ass pushing her into my face. I lick harder, waiting for her breathing to become labored. Her hands tug at my hair.

"Don't come."

"I. . ."

"Don't. Wait. Let the pleasure build," my firm voice fills the room.

Her knees clap to my head. She moves her hips to one side, then the other attempting to evade the erotic pleasure inside her.

"Ah," she moans, trying to push off the euphoria she's withering under.

I decide she can't take more of my teasing. My cock is poised over her opening and thrusts into her as she cries out, bursting with orgasms as she cries out my name. I pump her until she's had her fill, then climax, emptying myself into her.

22

LIAT

It's a new day in many ways. Riccardo left early, he kissed me before he left. Drowsy from sleep, I don't remember what time it was, only that the room was dark. I woke him with my nightmare. I remember him whispering softly to me that I was safe. Apparently, I was thrashing about and yelling in my sleep.

After being in that cellar, I won't take seeing the sunrise for granted. I stifle the thoughts of it when they pop into my head. I wonder if I'm doing the right thing by keeping it inside. I can't burden Riccardo with it. I want to be the fun in his life because he's serious enough for a dozen world leaders with the weight of the world on them. Aunt Vivian says that our Prime Minister aged decades in just two years of being in office. I believe it's from the stress now that I'm learning about the life Riccardo hid from me.

I dress with what I have, excited to get out of the house, but it's not without trepidation.

"Good morning," Francesca hands me an espresso as I enter the dining room.

"Thank you." I hold the cup and wonder how she knew I was up.

"How are you? We never talked about your ordeal. Riccardo is a wonderful man, but sometimes a woman needs another woman to talk to." She grabs a pan off the stove, dumps eggs on a plate, and we sit at the table.

"Thank you." I down my espresso, and the eggs are appetizing. I haven't been in the mood to eat. One meal a day is enough.

"Riccardo left me with strict instructions that you are to eat," she gives me a wry smile. "I can't say I disagree," she sips from a coffee cup on the table.

"Dancing burns up calories. It's a lifestyle, not a job. They are one and the same."

"Are you going back to it when this is over?" Her direct question takes me by surprise, and I scramble to discern her motives. Neutrality is golden.

"I don't know." I shrug. It feels like it's been months, not days, since I last danced. I've lost track of time, yet it hasn't bothered me.

"Don't overthink it. There are times when life moves fast, then too slowly. It will come about in time." She leans back in her chair and watches me before she texts on her phone.

I assume she's giving Riccardo an update.

I wonder what Francesca has been through to be so calm. She was there, in that room, with Riccardo, and she wasn't fazed by anything. The comments about her father last night at dinner were peculiar. It's like the family has an inside talk, and I lack the cliff notes to keep up.

"Who is your dad?" I nibble at the bacon on my plate, taking in how beautiful she is in a plain sweater and jeans. Her brownish-blond hair has streaks of warm blond, but her eyes are striking, reminding me of the bright green one might find if they caught a glimpse of an Aurora Borealis gracing the night sky.

"He was a Don, whacked beyond belief, as were my brothers. It's a long story," her matter-of-fact voice is chivalrous. I'm convinced there's more to the story. One day I will hear it, Riccardo will tell me eventually if I'm to be a part of the family.

"I guess we all are entitled to one of those, aren't we?" I finish eating, psyching myself up to leave the house and hope I won't be anxious around strangers. Shopping is fun, I haven't been on a spree in a long time. Just another day, that's all.

"Yes, we are. However, Enzo has the car warming up. We need to get you something to wear, but first, we're going to put on some new hair."

It didn't take long to get me fitted into a wig. I'm astounded by how different I look as a blond.

"There, now we can go, and the car will be warm," she speaks as she flips her fingers through her long, black hair.

"Finally, I get out of the country," my smile reminds me of how I used to be all the time.

"Yes. I can't wait to get home. Let's hope we get the information we need today to get out of here in a few days."

"I don't have any identification on me, how can I leave?"

"We'll make it happen; we always do." Francesca gives me a reassuring hug, and I'm grateful she's here, it could have been all men. She's the first woman I don't have to compete with for a spot with a dance troupe. I'm assuming she's with Sal, they are inseparable, a natural couple in my eyes.

The city is busy when we arrive. It's as if I never left, and we make our way to the large shopping mall. My hair bobs as I walk. I can pretend to be a woman without a past.

"Let's go in here," Francesca opens a door to a shop I know I can't afford. Even if I had access to my bank account, this store would be too dangerous for me to go into. Like Aunt Vivian used to say, 'if you have to ask the price, you can't afford it.

"It's pricey." I protest.

"Cost is not an issue. Riccardo is loaded. Have some fun. You're too young to be so serious. I know you went through an ordeal. That will never happen again."

Tentatively, I step inside the store, and the colors and designs are incredible. It reminds me of carefree days at school in Paris.

"I have rubles, we'll blend in like locals. Only speak to me in hushed tones, so we don't announce we're foreigners. We're here out of necessity as you can't be washing your underwear out every night. Remember that. Get what you need and a few extras."

I nod and follow her to the intimate wear where I pick out ordinary items, but notice Frances picks up sexy items in my size. We're roughly the same build, she must be surprising Sal tonight. Instinctively, she catches my eye and drops them in a carry-all tote and now it's obvious she's shopping for me, or rather, Riccardo when the crotchless underwear makes it into the tote.

"Mm," I murmurer at the glint in her eye. She's worldly, I can see how she could be with the men in camouflage pants and boots one minute and a sexy vixen the next. She adapts. I've seen her wield a weapon. She's important to the family, and I like her. It's nice to be around a woman who isn't pretentious.

Today, I get to experience her softer side. She's not one to show it often, and when she does, I know it's for Sal. I wonder if we've become friends.

We whisper back and forth as I try on jeans, sweaters, and shirts. I pretend we're affluent when she pays the bill when inside, I wonder how rich Riccardo really is, and I never knew that either. Francesca suggests we eat lunch after she picks up a cell phone for me to set up later with a data card, not on the Russian radar.

The mall is a destination spot for Russians because it house's a number of different eateries. One floor is dedicated to commercialized food chains found globally. I know Aleksandr and George loved to come here and held fond memories from their teenage years spent here and at the movie theater.

We're carrying our shopping bags as I gain my bearings with so many people passing by. I move closer to Francesca, when did I become afraid to be in crowded places?

I focus on the menu board in front of us, and a man is giving his order at the register, we're number seven in the queue. I know that figure, that shape. I look for the snake on his neck, and when I see it, the room spins.

Francesca slips her arm through mine, "Steady, Liat. I'll get you out of here. I think I made you do too much."

"No, it's him, the man with the snake tattoo. He beat me with the books," I whisper weakly.

She punches something on her phone and walks me calmly through the large entrance of the wall and into our waiting car. I slide in and lean my head back, afraid to pass out I fight it.

I hear the trunk close, and Francesca tells Enzo to drive slowly around the block and park a few blocks away. She'll text him to pick her up, and she closes the door.

"Where is she going?"

"We don't ask that, but I gather she's hunting someone."

"What do you mean?"

"Nothing. Just take a few breaths, you look like you saw a ghost."

"I wish. What I saw isn't fit for life on this earth."

I wish I weren't weak. I should have punched him, done something to hurt him like he hurt me. Instead, I'm too frail and don't know how to fight. I'm smart enough to know I can't risk the family mission to get this woman named Ignazio.

I drift in and out, like a fog over a lake, sometimes it's dense, and there is no vision, and other times, there are glimpses of water and land. Enzo drives, and Francesca gets in.

"Are you alright?"

It's not freezing at this time of day, but her cheeks are bright—her eyes show determination.

"That man is with Ignazio, I followed him. Killing him would announce our arrival. However, I managed to clone his phone, so we'll see what he's up to and where he lives. You did well back there. You held yourself together," she reaches for my hand, and I put mine in hers. She gives me a reassuring squeeze as she checks my pupils and feels my clammy forehead. "You'll be fine. We'll get you home."

I force myself to sit taller in the seat, not wanting to give in to the fear that grips me like a Python.

23

———

LIAT

"What do you mean he was there?"

I've never seen Riccardo so angry. He stalks the floor like a madman who needs sedation.

"I have his phone, it's great intel. What are the odds?" Francesca reasons with him, but Riccardo is beyond reasoning. He's out for blood.

"You did the right thing, I'm just livid Liat had to see him again."

"I'm here, Riccardo. I'm not a baby. It took me by surprise, that's all. I'm fine," I protest, sitting next to Francesca on the sofa.

"No, you're not. You're still traumatized. These situations can take years to recover from, and I don't want you ever to see him again." The look he gives Francesca tells me the man will be taken care of, as in killed. Dead. Riccardo's eyes are throwing enough daggers toward Francesca to cause her to plead her case rationally.

"The odds are a million to one," I state, interrupting her. "Besides, you said these people run the city, so it's only appropriate that they live here. Besides, Francesca cloned his phone," I end on a positive note, hopeful he'll simmer down.

Riccardo takes hold of my arm, "He'll never breathe the same air as you. Do you understand?" his gruff, possessive voice shakes me. His hand will leave a mark on my arm.

I pull back, "I'm not your property. I want to go home."

"You need me to get you out, and we can't do that until we finish here. Do you want to be on the run forever?"

"No," I reply meekly. "Of course not. I'm fine. You're fine. Let's find out what is on his phone."

All eyes in the room turn toward Francesca.

"We've used the men helping us here to read through it, and it appears that he is linked to Ignazio, so that's a plus. They were going to keep Liat and use her as bait for you, Riccardo. It confirms what we suspected. There were transfers of money as well."

"I'm not sure if he is with the Volkovs or if he's a mercenary for hire and reports to Ignazio directly," Massimo leans against the doorway with a snifter of cognac in his hand. "We also dropped the idea to Nikolay to check all of Ignazio's bank account."

"Yes, that is all setup. This will breed distrust between the couple," Dante solemnly agrees.

"What if he's thinking with his cock and not his brain?" Sal interjects.

Dante rolls his head back and then to the side as he observes his brother. "Let's hope that's not the case. He's the top man here, however, I'm sure there are others above him, or on his level, who wouldn't be happy to hear about a Russian that can't make his woman obey the laws of the Bratva. It comes first, and Valad would have to take care of it if it came down to it. Let's hope the new situation put pressure on him and Ignazio."

"Great. So, what do we do now?" I ask, anxious to get to the next phase of the debauchery.

"You're to go to bed," Riccardo states, his tone conveying the fact that I'm not to question him again.

"Fine," I huff, using it as my objection. I stand, knowing I have no say in the matter as they obviously have things to discuss, and they don't include me.

What is it about him that makes sense, even when I don't want it to?

I make my goodnights, and Francesca slips the new phone into my hand.

"It's encrypted and, on our system, no one can track you."

"Thank you so much." Finally, I have some support. I can't call anyone in Russia. I doubt Aunt Vivian knows Riccardo is here. Riccardo said he talked to her. He also told her she'd see me later this month.

I sulk in the bedroom, their voices outside are muffled, and there is a laugh here and there. I go through the bags from today and pull out the sexy lingerie. I'll show Riccardo that I'm not to be taken lightly. I know I drive him crazy.

I lay under the covers where I stream videos to get back in touch with the world. It's growing late as two hours have passed. The doorknob turns. I toss my phone on the nightstand.

"What a long day." Riccardo takes off his shirt and strips to his boxers.

I throw the covers back and roll onto my hands and knees as he takes me in, surprise registering in his eyes.

"I thought you might like to change things up," I

acknowledge his hard cock between us by reaching out and grabbing it, playing the part of a domineering woman.

"Hm. I see," he steps out of his underwear, moving closer. He notices my arm has a bruise where he grabbed me earlier.

He touches it tenderly. "I'm sorry. I was out of control. No one is to touch you or look at you without my say so. I'm serious."

"I know," I relinquish my defiance. How can I resist the virile man in front of me who only has my best interest at heart? "You have to keep me safe."

"I failed once, I can't fail again," his hazel-green eyes darken like the green grass of summer. He's not one to play around with, I've known this my entire life.

I'm beginning to understand why he's never had a life partner. He's been punishing himself all these years and living a solitary life.

"I bought this for you, Francesca thought you would like it," I run my hand over my ass covered in lacy panties.

He cups my breast, flicking his thumb over my nipple until it's excited and hard against his flesh. He kisses me softly, our lips merging as his tongue slips into my mouth. I part my legs as his hand runs up my inner thigh and touches my warm lips, inserting two fingers into me. I gasp with immediate pleasure. My crotchless panties would be wet if not for his expert finger fucking. My wetness coats him.

"You're excited for me," he breathes against my slender neck.

"Very," I whisper in his ear as I tug it between my teeth.

"I want to fuck you here, now." He pushes me backward, and I let myself fall onto the bed.

"I want you to fuck me," I pull his head to me, and our

lips meet with a feverish desire for more. I'll never have my fill of him no matter how many times we fuck.

His hard cock pressed against my labia briefly. Before I was prepared, he thrust his throbbing cock into me. I cry out in surprise and meld with the intense pleasure that courses through me. This is so hot. I'm turned on like never before, my nails dig into his solid biceps as I cling to him as he hammers into me thrust after thrust.

The friction builds quickly, the lacy panties adding to the friction on my clit, a bit of pain with the pleasure. I moan, and my head makes an arc when he pulls his cock out, I wrap my legs around him loosely and grab his toned ass, pulling him to me, and he pushes his cock into me again.

My pussy pulsates around his engorged cock as he moves hard and fast, he grabs my neck in his large hand, his fingers pressing on the side of my neck, making my orgasm rise to a peak. I remain in a tantric state. I move my hands to his throat, gripping him tightly, a glint of surprise fills his eyes, then a loud moan escapes him.

We're locked together as a final thrust breaks the spell. I shudder with an intense orgasm. I cry out as I come, clinging to him, as his hard body slams me one last time, his deep voice echo's off the bare walls, his body quivers as he comes, his rigid body remains over me, and his cock still fills me.

My heart races and my breathing returns to normal. Our bodies, damp with sweat, slide together as he slowly rolls off me, causing his seed to rush out of me.

"You fucking drive me crazy," he murmurs.

24

———

LIAT

I wake, and the bed is empty beside me. I can't expect Riccardo to live his life around me. I'm not that naïve. I feel my neck, then get up to see if he left any marks. He did not, but that was intense sex. I was afraid I might hurt him as his face turned red before he exploded in me. From the sound of his drawn-out growl and moan, I assume his orgasm was as intense as mine.

Call it intuition, but the neck thing was a bit kinky. I just followed his lead, thinking if it was good for me, it would be good for him. It appears we both have a parchment for some kinky sex. Why else would there be sex dens and strip clubs if men didn't like the thrill of something new or illicit?

Is that what I am to him? In all these years and our recent fucking, numerous times a night, when his hard cock pressed between my butt cheeks, waking me up, he's never uttered an emotional response.

He's a bit possessive, but I kind of like it. I'm sure he feels responsible for my kidnapping, but he rescued me. Doesn't that account for something?

I have no idea what they talked about tonight. Riccardo

toes the line, keeping his lips sealed on the family's secrets. I'm intrigued he went from being a man of the law to one who breaks it.

I have so many questions. I'm afraid to ask him for details. I've had time to observe the family, and I find Massimo and Sal are close, and I find it endearing. Their resemblance to each other can't be denied. Their disposition is not as aloof as Dante's, but he is the King and I'm sure he has to remain more detached than his siblings

I'm sure it's due to the hierarchy in the family business as he's not calloused towards his brothers. I'm sure he and Riccardo rely on each other to keep the family business afloat. Sal is a numbers man, Massimo and Francesca both have a stance that reminds me of Riccardo. I wonder what they do other than carry out assigned tasks.

This Ignazio, part of me wants to see her and the other half never wants to hear her name again. I've picked up pieces of information, but I may never hear the entire story. Some kind of feud is what I gather, and she killed a few loyal men. Mafia men. I have an inkling of why Dante became her target, but how did Riccardo get on her list?

I never imagined the words of hit lists, killing, and kidnapping to be talked about so freely. Who would have thought I'd be with a man in the mafia? Someone who holds life in his hands, and takes it? Am I crazy for wanting him? Is he ever going to admit he has feelings for me outside of the hot sex we have?

Does he have a woman stashed somewhere? I never asked.

I wash my face and wear my new clothes. They do make me look more mature but in a good way. I walk to the kitchen and hear the name Krill mentioned. When I appear, everyone stops talking.

I greet them, and Massimo hands me an espresso, then excuses himself as he buttons up to go outside. Sal follows.

"What are they doing?" I ask Francesca, who is dressed in camouflage clothing.

"We've set up a practice site."

"Practice site for what?"

"Drills together, don't be alarmed if you hear gunfire."

"Gunfire?" Now this, I've got to see. I've never held a gun, but I think it's time I do.

I gulp my drink and slide into my coat before I proceed to follow her outside like a puppy.

The ground is uneven, and my fancy boots get muddy.

Riccardo and Dante fire at handmade targets on the fence posts.

Riccardo's disposition changes when he sees me. He's all business without any semblance of affection. It's as if I'm not here until he hands me ear protection. I slide it over my ears and he promptly places a handgun in my hands.

He instructs me on how to slide it back to make it hot. I try and can't do it. He places his hand over mine and moves the slide showing me how it's done. He slides behind me, knocking my legs out with his foot so I'm in a stance to support myself against the kick of the forty-five in my hands. He's my body double, his frame towers over me. I embrace our closeness and the knowledge I've gleaned today. I wish I had this gun in the cellar.

Riccardo tells me to take a deep breath before I pull the trigger. I'm not sure what will happen when I do. I'm calm as Riccardo has my back and it reassures me I can do this. For now, it's enough. I pull the trigger and withstand the kick as my hand flies back, surprising me.

"Well done, Liat. Well done. Keep practicing. Now do it

on your own." Everyone on the impromptu range appears to have something on their mind. Something big.

"Great." I'm not sure of myself or my capabilities. Do I want the responsibility of a gun if I ever see the man with the snake tattoo? Or Timofey? He appears to be in the wind, but Francesca may have more information than she alluded to if the two men worked together. I know she cloned his phone. I'm sure it's for a reason. She doesn't mess around.

"So, what's up?" I ask Riccardo who pretends to not hear me before he walks off to be with Dante and Massimo.

"Don't get overly concerned. They've got a lot on their mind. They always work. You'll get used to it," she shrugs, walks two feet away from me, and starts shooting her gun. When she's out of ammo, she whips out a knife, throwing it faster than my eyes can follow. It hits the wood post under the target and remains in the post.

Wholly fuck. She's impressive. A chill runs up my spine. I think I've figured out what she does for the family. She hands me another gun and shows me how to load it. She shows me how to stand and makes me shoot again to practice. After a few magazines, I'm comfortable. I can see how this could be a turn-on.

Dante is behind me, talking with Sal when I pull my ear protection off.

"The oil company is the front for laundering money, not that he needs it, but to invest it in property, he has to move it around. Krill mentioned she likes to swim every day at the same time. No doubt, it's one of the few things she allows herself to do on a schedule as she has the public pool closed for her."

"Yes, we've checked it out, she's shown up there, and only one guard is with her. Valad never goes with her," Massimo rattles off in Italian. "He discovered money missing and had his men check her out, they were arguing. Things got heated, Enzo said. I think we're creating a keg that will explode."

I detect satisfaction in Massimo's voice and assume their plan is falling into place.

"Let's hope so, the sooner we leave here, the happier I'll be," Riccardo states.

"I'm sure my wife will appreciate that, too," Dante adds with confidence.

Riccardo is off to the side speaking to Enzo, I can't hear what they're saying. Enzo nods his head.

"What's going on?" I ask Riccardo who tells me to shoot the gun again. "It's nothing for you to worry about."

"Um. I see," only I don't. I have no clue what is going to transpire from one hour to the next.

"Really? What do you see?" his voice taunts me.

"I'm just a convenience to you. You tell me nothing," I point my gun to the ground for safety.

"I have a job to do, Liat. You can't speak to me this way in front of the others. We'll discuss it later."

"Now," I demand, quieter than normal.

"Later," he seethes, and it's evident I've crossed the line.

"Fine," I reply before shoving the gun into his hand and stomp back to the house alone.

I decide to make food for everyone as the house is empty. It will give me something to concentrate on other than the man outside who doesn't have time for me.

I try my best to not fret over Riccardo. It was not until now that I find myself longing for the comfort of dancing. This is the first time since being kidnapped that I felt the urge to return to what I love. It's a place where I know the boundaries and rules. I'm accomplished on the dance floor, not on a gun range. This is the first time in my life I've found I'm limited in what I can do outside of ballet.

I pull meat and cheese out of the old refrigerator and cut the loaf of bread on the counter. Someone must have picked it up this morning as it's fresh. Absentmindedly, I put items together making sandwiches and hope it will suffice.

At two, everyone comes in and finds the table set and food is on the table. I must have made Riccardo happy as he nodded to me as he washed up in the sink.

"Thank you for the food. It's very thoughtful of you," he nuzzles my neck gently.

"Happy to do it," I reply.

We sit next to each other at the table. I'm happy for our time together but I can't fight the regret I feel for not leaving Russia sooner. My life has been altered by the events of this week. For how long, I'm not sure.

I haven't learned how to read Riccardo's mood. I don't know where I stand or what I can expect from a man who's married to the "family." Maybe I'm not the marrying kind after all.

Do I want a man home for dinner at seven every night or one who is mysterious and silent? Can I be happy with a man who keeps half his life a secret from me?

We all eat and I can't follow the conversation. I'm lost in my own thoughts.

Later that night, I confront Riccardo on the exchange of our words outside.

"I'm a man the men look up to. I can't have you questioning me in front of them. Never again, Liat," his words sting. I'll never be special in his life. He's married to his family, and it doesn't leave room for me.

"I wish I had made my flight. I wouldn't be stuck here

without anything to do. I need to get back," I purse my lips together and fold my arms.

"You'll get back when you get back. Don't bring it up again. You should have left before I arrived, but you did your own thing, as usual. Now you can suffer the consequences. I'm not sure you're cut out for this life. You're used to the spotlight and doing what you want when you want to do it."

As much as I wanted him to placate me, he was right. In my defense, he could have filled me in. I might have listened. I can't deny I am used to getting what I want. I've worked hard and earned my stars. If it wasn't for my feelings for him, I'd say I'm right where I want to be at this point in my life.

The question is, does Riccardo want me in his life? Is he in love with me? Or, am I a convenience to him? Will he forget me when we return to Italy?

25

———————

RICCARDO

The next day, we gear up and head out after lunch. Enzo is staying behind to guard Liat at the house. Enzo adjusts the wire in his ear which connects him to John's men who patrol the vast grounds. Liat will undoubtedly pepper Enzo with questions; he'll remain silent.

"Are you and Liat okay?" Dante quizzes me as we walk to the van. He's on my list of people to keep happy. We're close, but even that has its drawbacks at times. "Your face is worth a million words, I just don't know which ones," he chuckles.

"Liat is not an easy woman, I'm not sure she's for me. She's opinionated, this new generation of women is foreign to me," I shrug.

I should feel bad for giving Liat a tongue-lashing earlier. In hindsight, it might be the only way she learns her place. This is a man's world unless she has a skill set valuable to us.

She's not used to sitting on the sidelines. In time, she must adjust, but do I want her to change for me?

"I should have smuggled Liat out through Belarus," I murmur as we're being driven to the public pool where we intend to kill Ignazio. "Neutralizing her bodyguard won't be difficult. Krill mentioned her henchmen are combing the local hideouts for word of us and offering a hefty bounty for information on our whereabouts. I'm glad we're out of the city," I sigh in relief.

"Getting Liat out was impossible. You can't trust men you need to hire for jobs. Mercenaries are only loyal to money, and who is currently paying them the most. This country is infiltrated by Russian spies. Liat could slip through your fingers again. Do you want that?" Dante's voice is edgy.

"Of course not," I bark. I can't discern if his new demeanor is due to me beating myself up over Liat's kidnapping, or if he's concerned over the mission at hand.

"I understand you want Liat to be safe. But she'll be secure at the house with Enzo. Men patrol the fences." Dante pats me on the back to reassure me.

"How long is it before John's men give us up once they hear of the bounty?" I ask.

"We'll be done tomorrow. I think we'll be fine. Besides, we've made our men happy and John is happy."

Fuck, I should have stayed behind, but I need to be the one to kill Ignazio. I need peace of mind. Francesca and Sal will make sure Ignazio is on her way to the pool before they surprise her other two mercenaries. The cloned phone provided more than enough information to find their apartments and friends.

We slow our approach to the public pool, an indoor facility, it's plain, one would easily miss the sterile gray exterior. There are only a few cars in the lot, so we take note of them and circle around.

Dante puts his earpiece in and announces, "She's on her way."

"I'll circle around again," Massimo replies as he pulls the van around.

"Good," Dante replies as he checks his gun and puts it in the clip on the back of his pants. He covers it with his large shirt. We have other soldiers as lookouts on the off-chance Ignazio anticipates us being here with reinforcements who might be alerted.

I update Sal and Francesca over our cell phones as we wait for her black Mercedes to arrive.

"Right on cue, I don't know if I trust it," Dante comments as the car approaches.

"Right. Me either, but this is it, or we'll have to come back. We can't stay off the grid forever. I wouldn't be surprised if she knows we're here. What are the odds she has men hidden inside?"

"That's anyone's guess," Massimo chortles. "I'll be behind you as look out and remain in touch with the men outside."

I slide the van door open, and Dante is one step behind me as we approach the gym carrying a bag that makes us look like we're here for a swim. It's always good to remain inconspicuous.

The woman at the check-in desk is gone. The place was quiet until I hear Ignazio give directions to her bodyguard. He's to remain in the pool area as no one can get into the locker room from the back. We researched the facility, the doors are in the front, and on the other side of the building is the exit route from the gym.

We push into the pool area, the guard turns to us, unsuspecting, and I shoot him in the head using a silencer. We wait for our nemesis.

She doesn't disappoint as she enters the pool area in a black one-piece swimsuit, wearing a swimming cap. It makes sense with the weather and the fact she does this every day, no doubt the water would compromise the integrity of her hair. The hair she's always coloring to blend in around the world. No one can accuse her of sacrificing her vanity even if she's a hardened serial killer.

"I see you've arrived at last. You didn't have to kill Igor," she eyes her guard bleeding out on the pool decking.

"What's the endgame?" Dante asks as he holds his gun on her.

"Hm, well, while you're here, I have another surprise planned. You kill me, I kill Liat," she smiles like the piranha minus the extra teeth.

Her words leave a sting. My skin burns with rage. I'm not taking the bait. I have faith in Enzo.

"Did you hear that?" I speak into the mic that goes to Massimo.

"Oh, that won't work. I've jammed all transmissions."
Fuck. Of course.

"It seems we're at a stalemate," she moves closer to the water.

"Stop where you are," I warn holding the gun on her. "What do you want?"

"To make you all vulnerable. I never expected our paths to cross, Riccardo. Once I found you, I couldn't let you off easily. Your team killed my lover in Israel. I took over as the Phantom. It's easy to do when the real one with any digital footprint is dead. And eye for an eye. Only you were to be in the car that day."

"You fucking bitch!" I squeeze the trigger, and as she falls, the gun concealed behind her hits the tile with a clink. I thought I'd experience rage from the incident, however, I find I'm relieved. The past is closed. She's dead, the loop has been closed for me, Dante, and Juliet.

I don't have time to process the obscure circumstances leading to our paths crossing so many years later. She's a tenacious adversary.

"Riccardo, Liat is in danger, we'll never make it there in time."

"Let's round up Massimo. We'll have a signal and divert Francesca and Sal," he yells as we race from the building.

Dante shoots the lens on the outside security cameras and I toss an incendiary bomb into the building as we exit, keeping our heads low. No doubt the place will be flooded by the Russian police. It will keep the Governor busy as he wonders where his partner is, and upon discovering she's dead, he'll cover this up. They always do. His own men might even suspect him of killing her as her bank accounts are filled with money Sal transferred to them.

Massimo pulls up in the van and we hop in. Francesca calls me and I use the speaker on my phone so we can all hear her update. She and Sal found the first flat of the thugs, and it was cleared out. Instinctually, they immediately headed to the safe house.

"It's not so safe anymore." I yell into the phone and tell Massimo, "Step on it."

"We can't get pulled over," Massimo complains as he maneuvers around slow traffic while Dante keeps his eyes focused on cars that might have markings of police who could intercept us.

"So far, we're in the clear," I say leaning forward in the front seat and pushing my foot into the floorboards. "I'm sure the mess back there will have security forces dispatched in the other direction. Just get me to Liat!" Sweat drips from my brow, my hands are clammy.

"I'm on it!" Massimo yells as he checks the mirrors and forces the van to go faster than it's ever been driven.

"Fuck, what if Liat doesn't make it? It's not good, Dante." I'm a nervous wreck thinking the worst.

"You can't assume the past will continue to repeat itself. You rescued her from the kidnappers, we can do it again. You must have faith. Besides, for being so damn petite, she can be quite lippy. And this time, she won't have her hands tied behind her back."

"Enzo won't go out without a fight," Massimo yells over the roar of the engine and the noise from the bumps we fly over due to the worn roads filled with potholes. We cover the countryside like a bat escaping captivity.

I grab the dashboard, I'm too nervous to buckle it. I pray this old van can get us back to the house in time.

26

LIAT

I'm pacing the floor and fear I'll wear out the area rugs and the wooden floors. I'm a bundle of nerves worrying over Riccardo. Today is the day, I know this because of the secretive talks, the practice out back yesterday, and that Riccardo and Francesca showed me how to shoot a gun.

I shouldn't have let him leave without words of encouragement. What if he's wounded and I never see him again? I've been a dolt for not telling him I love him and that his age and occupation don't matter.

What if he rejects me? When we're in bed, he's a different person, some rough sex for sure, it's exciting, and we both get off on it. But is that all we are? Fuck buddies?

My private debate is interrupted as AR15's are fired at the gate and I know someone must be crashing through. Everyone is gone, except for men who are out on patrol, and that means they aren't close enough. I run behind Enzo who is peering through the window in the door.

My heart is racing, I scramble to breathe.

Enzo pushes me behind him, "Get back. Stay down,

there's a gun in the kitchen and knives. Most of the team is in the city."

"Okay, I'll get it." I hunch down and make my way to the kitchen as gunfire permeates the walls of the house. Vases shatter sending glass into the living room, the trigger I hear clicking in the house means Enzo is firing back. We're outmanned. I cock the pistol. It's no match for the machine gun.

"How many men, Enzo?"

"Two, in a truck," he gasps.

I crawl across the floor, he's lying on it, jamming another cartridge in his weapon.

"You're hurt," I yell.

"I'll live," he grunts.

"Get back, we'll hole up in the kitchen." I grab his shoulders, knowing he's too heavy for me to drag but I manage to do so. He's firing at the door as we slip away from it for cover.

Adrenaline courses through my veins. I'm ready this time. No son of a bitch is ever taking me again. I cock the gun to make sure it's ready to go, we're on the floor of the narrow kitchen. Knives, yes, Francesca said they are even more dangerous than guns.

I rise into a hunched position and survey the counter as I locate the wood block filled with knives. I leap, grab it and hold it to my chest as I fall to the floor.

The front door crashes in. Frantically, I dump the contents of the knives on the floor and give some to Enzo. I have no clue what most of these are used for, but we're on a farm and the meat cleaver is heavy, and it gives me a better chance of hitting a target.

"Liat, give yourself up and we'll let your guard live," a familiar voice looms closer.

"I have a few bullets left, when I fire, throw the hatchet. There are two of them," he says as blood from his leg seeps onto the oiled wood planks.

I nod. I'm too afraid to say a word. It's as if not speaking will keep me hidden. But that's what children think of monsters. These monsters are real as the heavy boots move steadily towards us.

Enzo begins to fire in the direction of the attacker. But we've underestimated them as a man appears behind me and he'll grab me in a few seconds. We couldn't anticipate the man cutting across the living room on the other side of the wall.

Enzo's gun clicks but nothing comes out. He clicks. No ammo. It's then that I identify Timofey approaching us from Enzo's left. I grab the meat cleaver and heave it toward his chest. The look of shock on his face is priceless. I experience a moment of triumph as it sticks in his chest. Dancers have core strength; I might look petite and helpless but fuck him.

I hear a growl and words in Russian before I'm nabbed by my shirt and as I'm being pulled on my back, Enzo hollers my name, but he can't walk.

"I knew we'd meet again," the voice sends shivers up my spine.

He pulls my arm to make me stand, a gun rests against my temple. It's a handgun.

"Fuck you," I yell as I pull my arm up, gun in hand, point it toward his chin, and squeeze the trigger.

The blast makes my ears ring, but he reels backward and falls. The shock and rage of being beaten take over. I want him dead. I step towards him, and fire again, in his chest.

"Fuck you," I scream at him as he gasps for air. His gun lies at my feet.

Enzo! I turn back to the kitchen and Timofey is on his stomach laying over Enzo's feet.

I grab Enzo again, he clutches my arm and half rises, gimping away from our intruder. I sit him in a chair and rush to the kitchen to get towels and make a tourniquet, like in the movies. I have no clue if it will help but it keeps my mind occupied.

"Good girl," his voice is faint, but the blood isn't flowing as fast.

"Let's get you to the couch so we can get your leg up."

"Sure," he responds. He's weak and I worry the others won't be here in time to save him. I have no idea who to call.

Riccardo. I find my phone on the kitchen floor covered in Enzo's blood, my hands shake as I dial Riccardo.

"Dead, men. Enzo's hurt. He lost a lot of blood."

"Liat! We're on our way. There's a packet in the false bottom of my suitcase, it's a powder, it says hemostat on it. It will stop the blood from leaking out."

"Got it." I drop the phone to retrieve the packet for Enzo, but I can't locate the compartment Riccardo spoke of. I savagely feel around inside Riccardo's suitcase for the false bottom and in frustration, I turn his luggage upside down, then, pry the bottom up with my fingers breaking my nails in the process. I feel something and grab it.

I rush the packet to Enzo, rip it open with my teeth, and pour it into Enzo's bleeding leg. He yells, his face was pale before but lacks any color now. I hope I didn't kill him. A minute later, his wound is stable, clotting off and he opens his eyes.

"Thank you," His voice is thready. I assume he's in shock, but he's alive.

Vehicles skid across the dirt outside, and car doors are

slammed. I'm not sure who it is as I slump next to Enzo. My body shakes, my nerves; raw.

"Liat, Liat!"

Riccardo! He's here.

He's a vision as he runs over the smashed door, his face looks like he saw a ghost. He scoops me into his arms.

"I got here as fast as I could," he kisses my dirty face. I wrap my arms around him, relieved he made it home.

"Ignazio?"

"Gone."

"So are the men who took me. I can't believe snake guy had a semi-automatic to my head, like on my skin. It won't fire, Francesca told me, so I used it as my moment to pull my gun up and I shot him in the chin and stomach."

He pulls me to him, so tight I can't breathe. "Good girl. I'm proud of you. And what of the other?"

"Enzo got him first."

"Wholly shit," Massimo yells. "Did you really throw a meat cleaver? You're too small to sling that mother fucker."

"I might be a ballerina, but I'm quick on my feet."

Everyone laughs breaking the air filled with sweat, blood, and gunpowder.

"I guess this is a lot of damage," I murmur as Riccardo releases his grip on me.

"We'll give John enough money to rebuild it all," Dante smiles, and pats my back. "Well done, Liat. Well done."

Francesca catches my eye, and winks. "So, you're more than a ballerina. Is this beginner's luck or do you have talents we don't know about?"

"I don't know. I just want to get home and have a vacation," I breathe out in one swoosh before I crumple into Riccardo, the adrenaline wore off minutes ago.

Massimo brings me clear alcohol to drink. "To steady your nerves," he says.

I take the tiny glass, toss the liquid back, cough, and wipe my mouth as it burns going down.

Massimo grins, I've earned his respect.

"WHAT MADE you think you could toss a knife?" Riccardo quizzes me.

"Francesca and I made use of our girl time. It appears she bonds best over weapons," I snicker.

"True." He grins.

"So, what now?" I ask curling up in bed. The men spent hours digging holes for the bodies. I doubt anyone will miss them. Sal mentioned they had cleared out their flats, so I assume they were planning to leave.

"Now," he sits beside me, his feet firmly on the ground. "You need to rest."

"I'm sorry I was rude to you."

"It's over. Everything is over."

My heart sinks. We're over?

"The past is behind us, it's time for a new chapter."

"And what is that?"

"I think we need to take a long vacation, maybe get married on the French Riviera, Greece. Who knows? Anywhere you want to go."

"I'd follow you anywhere, but I need to know if you'll ever share your thoughts with me. I'd like to be in some of them."

His hands caress my face, he tilts my chin so I have to meet his gaze, "Liat. I've been a fool keeping you in the dark.

I love you. You are the only woman who has me mesmerized. As long as you'll have me, I'm yours."

A tear slips from one eye, then the other. He loves me! I haven't been in this alone after all.

"What? No sass out of that mouth of yours?" he teases.

"I love you, too."

His lips are gentle on mine and deepen into a kiss that conveys how vulnerable he is and that, even though we are different, it's nothing we can't overcome.

"Let's go home," I murmur against his warm lips as my nipples protrude through the sheer night dress I'm wearing.

"We leave before daylight, but first, I'm making love to you. I thought I lost you today."

"I thought I lost you, too. I just reacted without thinking."

"I want you to remember everything about tonight," he trails kisses down my neck. "It will be a long time before I let you out of my sight."

"I was planning on that," I smile as he leans over me and we sink into the bed.

27

———

LIAT

Krill met us at the airport with my passport and ID as a sendoff gift. I couldn't be more relieved to be going home. I had no wish to see Aleksandr as he betrayed me, but I understand the situation he was under. Dire times call for drastic measures. I'm not sure what I would have done if I had been in that situation. I'm hoping he would have alerted someone when I didn't resurface, but I'll never know.

Riccardo slips his hand through my arm as we board Dante's private jet, which has been waiting to take us home in style.

"Well, I assume you two can get married now." Riccardo ambushes Sal and Francesca as we drink champagne inside the plush jet, having just toasted the demise of the family's enemy.

"As soon as she gives me a date, it's a done deal," Sal beams, and I catch him winking at his fiancé.

"Great, I have this place picked out in Greece, it over-looks the water. The tables will be outside, overlooking the

Mediterranean Sea. Poles covered in live greenery will hold the chandeliers over the elegant tables, making it so pristine. What can be more beautiful than the view, the ambiance, and the entire family together in one place for a joyous occasion?"

"Really?" Sal's surprised voice catches our attention, "I didn't know you even thought about it."

"Why wait? We're not getting any younger, and all this traveling around has been a bit much. I'm ready for a nice long honeymoon," she purrs.

"I'm not complaining," he replies, dropping a kiss on her perfectly outlined lips.

"Great, give us the date. I'll get security lined up. I've learned I can never let my guard down," Riccardo raises his flute of champagne, "to the next bride and groom, may you live in love and prosper."

"Salute," everyone chimes in as glasses clink.

We arrive in Italy; the warm air adds to the glow in my cheeks that is fed by Riccardo making love to me every night. A limo van drives the Micheli family home. Riccardo mentioned the rest of the crew came home on commercial flights. Riccardo has a limo waiting for us.

"Fancy, Riccardo," I murmur. "How is it I'm only in a limo when I'm with you?"

As he sits back in the leather seat, surprise shows on his face, "I didn't know you required it, Liat."

"I don't, but it's pretty awesome," I take a sip of my drink when we're situated inside. I can get used to this.

"I'll tell you later how you can show your appreciation," his voice deepens, and his eyes hint at something naughty. I can't imagine what he might have in store for me. I'm excited wondering about it.

"My house needs a woman's touch. I hope you're up to the task. I also have a trusted man, Lorenzo, who will be your personal guard. He lives in his own wing of the house; he's been instructed to keep you on a short leash. I'm not taking any chances," he bends slightly to kiss my lips before lifting the bottle, "More?"

"Yes, please," I take the flute from him and watch the bubbles rise in the golden liquid. I'm floating, just like them. I don't ever want this bubble to burst, it's so surreal. Riccardo, the man who never cracked a smile, is as gregarious as I've ever seen him.

"Are you ready for the next chapter?"

I can't keep my eyes off him as I take in his scruffy jawline, his eyes dance with a flicker of life—a flicker which is long overdue. My face is aglow now that most of the bruises have faded, and I hope I don't remind him of the events we buried in Russia.

"I'm always up for a new challenge. I need to get back in shape. I think you packed a few pounds on me."

"You'll work them off," he states without hesitation.

"I bet I will." I finish my champagne, I'm a bit tipsy but happy.

"Do you mind being with an older man?"

"It depends on whether we have a future or not. What do you want?"

"I want you happy," his fingers run down the side of my face as he stares into my eyes. I can't escape his gaze; the one that leaves me naked. I can't lie to him. I can't hide my love for him.

"I'm not going to pick out your ring, so that will be a joint venture. My intentions are honorable. No one is ever going to put a hand on you. No one will know what it's like to be with you the way I am. I will be the only man you'll sleep with as long as I live."

The direct order is not taken lightly. He's a possessive man who knows what he wants. Saying yes to him is a commitment I will never be able to break. I know he'd never stop searching for me. He's vulnerable where I'm concerned. My panties are moist as he moves closer to me on the bench we share.

"Only you hold the power to make me forget the world around us. In all the darkness, you are my light. Will you be my wife, Liat?"

My breath catches in my throat. This is the largest decision of my life. The love I see in his eyes makes my heart to skip a beat.

"Of course, Riccardo. But I won't be in the dark on everything."

"I thought you wanted to go to New York and be on Broadway."

"I'm burned out and not ready to return. Your idea of a honeymoon is just what we need to spend time alone. Will Aunt Vivian approve?"

"Leave her to me. If I know her, she already knows."

The limo stops in front of a two-story house with green shutters. A handsome man greets us, introductions are made, he's my personal bodyguard.

"Will life settle down now that we're home?" My eyes glance around the first floor as we enter. It needs updating and screams man cave. I will have fun fixing it.

Lorenzo disappears to make us an espresso, for which I'm grateful as I'm tired between the travel, too much champagne, and my need for food.

"I have one question for you."

Riccardo stops on the steps to the second floor. "What?"

Standing beside him, I pause on the step, "What do you think about kids?"

"Kids, hum?" A corner of his mouth turns up as he pretends to ponder the question.

"Yes, I have to know," I take a deep breath, ready to make my case for them.

"I think this house needs more laughter than we can muster," and he swings me up into his arms and carries me to the landing as I squeal in delight.

"Wait until you see the playroom," his sultry voice chimes.

"You have a playroom for them already?" I ask in confusion.

"No, my love, it's one for us," he replies before he ravages my neck and carries me down the hallway.

FRANCESCA WAS the most impressive bride Greece has ever seen. Having her own mafia organization in southern Italy, she spared no expense on her gown. The white silk was an A-frame dress, with a thin strap over each shoulder, and a plunging V neckline, all covered with flower petals. The detailed beading was hand-sewn and accentuated her thinner waistline. The bottom was made of tulle, fell naturally around her hips, and extended into a train behind her.

Juliet and Dante were the perfect Groomsman and maid-of-honor. If Riccardo didn't tell me Juliet was expecting, I would have never guessed. I assume an announcement will be made when the bride and groom return from a honeymoon abroad. The details haven't been revealed.

Our wedding will occur in July, in typical Italian fashion with a limo ride for the entire wedding party to the Michelangelo statue overlooking the Pointe Vecchio bridge. I run a hand over the front of my salmon-colored dress to smooth it. We weren't looking to have kids right away, but Riccardo seems to have excellent swimmers because I think I'm pregnant. All it takes is not using birth control once. I'm not upset. In fact, I'm waiting for an official confirmation before I tell Riccardo. I'd hate to disappoint him if the home test wasn't accurate.

The work on the house has kept me busy, the trip to Russia has been forgotten, and I welcome the thought of a son or daughter running down the halls of our old house as it undergoes needed renovations. I can't part with the marble flooring, nor would I want to, it adds charm to the villa and keeps the house cooler in the summertime. The kitchen has been upgraded, and the extra bathrooms will be next, along with a nursery. I'm excited. Dance used to be my world but now it's Riccardo and the life we're building together. I never imagined my life being married to a mad man. His hours are deplorable, especially when he disappears into the night, leaving me to worry. I've been blessed that he's home before I wake up, and he insists on sending me with Juliet to buy a new wardrobe fitting my stature in my life.

I'm not one to make a huge fuss over fashion, preferring the arms of my lover over any trinket he uses to pacify me, or uses to seduce me. Aunt Vivian wasn't shocked by our engagement. It brought us closer in the respect that I'm officially family, not that my new last name is the deciding factor. I think she's happy I'll be staying in Italy and that my worldly escapades have slowed to a halt. Except for a honeymoon, I don't feel the need to traipse all over the world. I'm quite content with growing our family and kissing Riccardo every morning and every night. As long as he's by my side, I can't go wrong.

Prende and Valentina are interesting women in their own right. Valentina can get into spirited debates and run off in Sicilian dialect with Massimo. They seem to enjoy it, and I'm sure they settle any argument with time well spent between the sheets. I catch them passing secretive looks across the Sunday dinner table, and I have no doubts about them.

Prende is an outsider like me, she's of Albanian descent, but the family welcomes her. With Massimo being half Albanian and half Italian, the Micheli family has broken with the tradition of only Italian wives. I'm still learning each couple's history as I forge my own place with the family.

Mamma is still adamant about Sunday dinners. The sight of the men smoking cigars under the trees reminds me of a scene one would expect from the Godfather movies set in times past. There is much to be said for tradition. Here, we're blending the past with the present as time never stands still.

Riccardo hopes we're over all the unnecessary excitement for years to come, and I agree. But I'm a realist, and even though I'm young, I know life has a way of bringing us challenges and new beginnings. Together, we'll weather all storms.

Riccardo takes my hand and leads me to the small area where the wedding guests are slow dancing. He murmurs, taking me in his arms, "This is the first time we're dancing together."

"It won't be the last," I smile as I nuzzle up to his clean-shaven cheek and breathe in his scent mingled with his cologne.

He holds my hands in his, pulling them to his chest as he gazes into my eyes. "I love you, Liat."

"I love you too, sweetheart, this is a lovely wedding. And we get to see Greece."

"That's if I let you out of the bedroom," he teases.

"I'm sure we'll see some of the country," I jest.

"For sure, then it will back to the daily grind. But work doesn't consume me like before. Thank you for that."

What he means is that he's forgiven himself for the losses in our past. We're moved on.

"We need to see as much as we can now," I continue, "One never knows when there might be tiny feet walking the vineyard on our estate."

"Sure, I can't wait. Wouldn't it be nice for Dante's child and ours to grow up as cousins?"

"It would be amazing to say the least," I smile, knowing he sees through me.

"Whenever it happens is a blessing. It's more than I could have ever hoped for just a few short months ago," and with that, he drops a warm kiss on my painted lips.

"Amen, to that," he replies as he twirls me out, then pulls me back into his strong arms where I belong.

I hope you enjoyed this series! I loved all the characters! Please continue reading with King's Promise An Arranged Marriage Romance (Volkov Bratva).

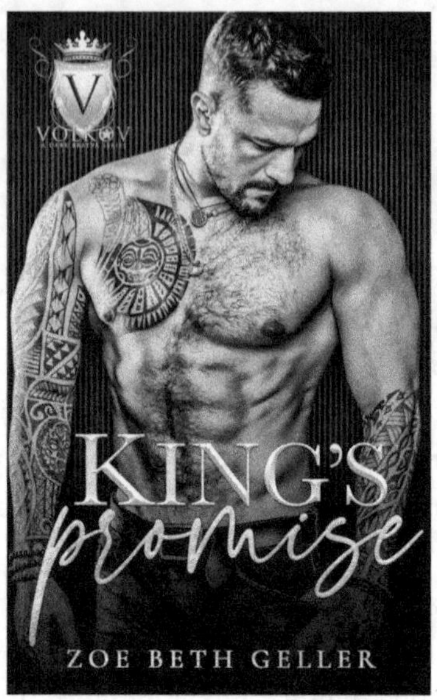

The prequel to King's Promise is a FREE new book on the next page!

FREE NEW BOOK!

FREE Book!

Https://geni.us/BratvaBride
Bratva's Bride

ALSO BY ZOE BETH GELLER

Dirty: A Dark Mafia Romance Series

Dirty: A Dark Mafia Romance Series (Micheli Mafia)

Italian King: A Dark Mafia Romance (Micheli Mafia)Book 1

Dirty Vengeance: A Dark Mafia Romance (Micheli Mafia) Book 2

Dirty Bargain: A Dark Mafia Romance (Micheli Mafia) Book 3

Dirty Born: A Dark Mafia Romance (Micheli Mafia) Book 4

Dirty Series Dark Mafia Fan Group

Dirty Deals: A Dark Mafia Romance (Micheli Mafia) Book 5

New Box Set

Micheli Mafia: A Dark Mafia Box Set

Volkov Bratva

King's Promise: An Arranged Marriage Romance

Brutal Promise

Mafia Reader/Fan Group on FB

Maine Megaladons (Football Series)

Faking it with the Football Star

Maine Maulers Series

Maine Maulers Hockey Series

Rookie in Love (now in audio)

Jagged Ice

Hotter than Puck

Benched by the Nanny

Puck in the Oven

Pucking the Team Captain

Sin Bin Hockey Series

Tyler: Hooked (Free prequel to the series)

The Sin Bin Hockey Series

Jackson: Against the Boards

Alan: Between the Pipes

Erik: Fire and Ice

Blayze: Slap Shot

Paavo: The Defender

Spencer:Penalty Box

Isak: Coach

Kaden: Game Time

Liam: The Enforcer

Jake: Roughing

The Sin Bin Hockey Series Box Sets

The Sin Bin Hockey Series Box Set Books 1-4

The Sin Bin Hockey Series Box Set Books 5-7

The Sin Bin Hockey Series Box Set Books 8-10

Zoe Beth Geller's Hockey Pond Fan Group

ACKNOWLEDGMENTS

Thank you to everyone who is following me on this journey. I hope you are enjoying this series. Special thanks to my hubby for his support.

ABOUT THE AUTHOR

I live in SWFL Florida with my grown kids and grandkids. When not writing I enjoy swimming, cooking, family nights and watching my son play ice hockey. I've kinda become the team mom which is cute because my kids aren't 'kids', they are adults!

I am the author The Sin Bin Hockey Series which is a collection of 10 standalone novels. There is a bit of continuity across books and they do not need to be read in order.

My second series, Maine Mauler Hockey Series, is a pro team series based, obviously, in Maine! These are interconnecting romances that can be read as standalone, but due to the interaction between players and a series arc it is best if you read it in order.

Other works include my dark mafia -The Dirty Series: A Dark Mafia Romance (Micheli Mafia). This was inspired by my love of Italy and I've visited family there many times. It's my home away from home. This series starts off with Italian King. These books should be read in order as the plots and romances are involved and carry through with the murder, mystery and suspense plot. This is a five (5) book series. Book one is not as dark as it gets, it all builds. Book two is femme fatale because Francesca spoke to me and took off. If you know my books you'll know it's like a rollercoaster. Set up, get to the peak and then the Whoosh to the end. But this romantic suspense series builds as a murder mystery, as well as a thriller, with tension and plot expanding with each book! I consider this a Steamy Contemporary romance where the mafia aspect grows and grows. Some characters and scenes are darker than others.

Want to sign up for the low down on my progress on the next work in progress? Want to join contests and enter for giveaways? Hockey fans can sign up here and get Tyler free. If you just want to sign up you can do so here.

What to be an ARC reader? Sign-up for my ARC! You can do hockey or mafia or both. It's like shopping, tons of options!

I love the reader (fan) groups! It's a place I drop in on most days and get to know my readers, hockey fans and mafia readers! If mafia is your jam, you can sign up here Newsletter sign-up

Fan Groups
Zoe Beth Geller's Hockey Pond
The Dirty Series: Dark Mafia Romances

Follow me on TT at zoebethgellerauthor1

ZBG Website

www.ingramcontent.com/pod-product-compliance
Lightning Source LLC
Chambersburg PA
CBHW060416310726
48976CB00003B/1073